Needs

Work

First Printing: 2019
ISBN-13: 978-1-942086-13-0
PL-125

Paragraph Line Books
Oakland, California

www.paragraphline.com

This novel is dedicated to my sister Nancy.

Needs Work

a novel

by

John L. Sheppard

Paragraph Line Books 2019

"Take a walk through the land of shadows

Take a walk through the peaceful meadows

Don't look so disappointed

It isn't what you hoped for, is it?"

— *Talking Heads*

TO THE READER.

Your friendly acceptance is all that is expected.

Mr. J.L. Sheppard.

POLICE INTERCEPTOR

I was let go.

That was months after my wife threw me out, taking our daughter with her. I was twenty-seven and starting all over again with life. I moved in with my father. Moved back to Ohio, a place that I thought I'd left in the rearview mirror. Instead, it was in my cracked and hazy windshield.

My car, a ten-year-old Ford Mustang, broke down in my father's driveway never to recover. It had thrown a rod.

I got out of the car. The parking brake popped. The car slowly rolled into the street. A small fire crackled under the hood. In few minutes, dark black smoke poured out from the undercarriage and a red glow simmered within the passenger compartment. For a moment, I saw a shadow behind the wheel, a remnant of my former self, the one who was so confident that he would never again grace the state of Ohio. A small explosion. Another small explosion. They sounded less like explosions than someone manually popping a paper lunch sack. The driver's side front wheel fell off and the car tilted over. The Mustang emblem clinked onto the pavement. A car, and then another car, drove past as if this sort of thing happened all the time. Nothing to get excited about.

"My clothes are in there," I said aloud. "My employee of the month certificate. My Army uniforms. My crazy pills."

My father emerged from the tiny house I'd grown up in, leaning forward on an aluminum walker, a wry grin on his mossy face. There was a reason why he'd never grown a beard while my mother was alive. The beard was patchy in so many ways. The coloration was wrong. The growth was uneven. There were too many things wrong with his beard to list.

The look he sent my way told me that he hadn't yet forgiven me for not coming around while my mother was dying. I came to the funeral. Wasn't that enough?

The police arrived. They pulled their cruiser up to the curb. A decal on the side of the car read, POLICE INTERCEPTOR. An older fat patrolman strolled up to me. He stood alongside me in silence and we watched my car burn for a while. Finally, he said, "That yours?" His name tag said, SMITH.

"Yes," I said. "I have no money."

"Who does?" He patted me on the shoulder solicitously.

The flames licked the air. It was sensuous.

"This is my son." My father was beside us, opposite the cop.

"Total loss," the friendly, gray-haired patrolman said. He rubbed his belly like there was a cat underneath his shirt.

His partner, a youngish woman, her hair pinched into a severe bun at the nape of her neck, stood near the car in the street, waving other cars past. When the street was clear, she pulled out her ticket pad and wrote me up.

My state of Illinois vanity plate fell off the back. It read, "E4MAFIA." It was a joke that wasn't funny now that I was out of the Army. I'd been out of the Army for years. I was in the Army for four years, most of it spent in a Navy hospital in Illinois, recovering from my war wounds. The Navy corpsmen would wheel us all up to the roof of the hospital at times, I remembered. We'd sit up there, high above the base, staring at Lake Michigan. It was calming. The hospital specialized in traumatic brain injuries. It was why we were all there. We were learning to speak again. To feed ourselves. To walk. To read and write. The Navy's corpsmen school was there, so the student corpsmen would come by to gawk at us, or help us out with basic things. Eating. Finding our way back to our ward.

The female cop put away her ticket book, picked up the plate and then dropped it. "Hot," she said. She crinkled her brow and wiped her burnt hand on her pants leg.

"Of course it was hot," my father said. My father wasn't an old man. He was only sixty-five. But a lifetime of hard labor had destroyed his body, left him without a couple of vertebra in his back and a raw spinal cord. My father built things with his hands, mostly walls, mostly out of bricks, rocks and mortar. It all depended on the job.

When I was a child, and up into my late teens, I went with him on jobs, when school didn't interfere. I remember eating sandwiches that my mother made for him. She loved yellow mustard and dill pickles. Sometimes, that was all that was on the sandwiches.

The Mustang went up in a whoosh, pushing us all backward. The female cop ended up on her keister. She got back up, none the worse for wear, and walked over to the driveway where we were all standing. "Total loss," she noted.

"Yeah," Smith said.

"Ticket?" she asked me.

"Um," I went, puzzled by the question. If there was an option, I did not want to take it.

She handed me the ticket with a slight shrug. I looked down at what she'd written. In a box labeled OTHER: "Public nuisance." "Fair enough," I said.

"That's your court date," she said, pointing it out with a well-honed fingernail lacquered in glittery polish. She had huge eyes that dominated her face. She wore bright pink lipstick. She was half a head shorter than me. Her name tag said, JONES. "Here. Have a flyer." She handed me a sheet of paper, eight-and-a-half by eleven. REPORT ALL STRAYS, it said at the top. In the middle of the sheet, there was a photo of a man with slicked back hair and a well-trimmed Van Dyke. I tipped the paper and the photo morphed into a bulgy-eyed chihuahua. At the bottom: $100 REWARD.

"I'll let you know if I see any," I said. "Strays."

Smith was half a head taller than me. He grabbed me around the shoulders from behind and gave me a shake. "Attaboy." The Cleveland Police Department is not known for this sort of encouragement, so he was exceeding my expectations.

My car had burned to the ground. There was little left now. Lumps of unshiny metal glowed in the street.

"Welcome home, son," my father said. He turned to the white cop and shook his hand. "Larry Derleth." He turned to the black cop and shook her hand. "Larry Derleth," he said again. "My son is being rude. His name is Phillip. Phil, shake their hands."

"Phil Derleth." I shook each of their hands in turn.

"Don't forget your court date," Officer Jones said. "You wanna…?" she went to her partner, tilting her head toward their car.

"Oh… sure. Excuse me," Officer Smith said.

"Yes," Officer Jones said. "We beg your pardon."

"Such a beautiful day otherwise," Officer Smith commented. He looked skyward to demonstrate.

"Indeed," Officer Jones said, glancing skyward. "It is indeed a beautiful day."

The two of them strolled over to the police interceptor, opened their respective doors and casually entered the vehicle. The two doors slammed shut. Jones turned on the siren and lights for a moment, and then turned them off. The engine roared to life and the tires chirped on the hot pavement. Off they went.

"We can clean up later," my father said. He nodded toward the house. "C'mon. I've fixed dinner. There's plenty for the both of us."

I trailed behind him to the house. The scent of burning rubber and axle grease followed us. A stack of waffles sat on a plate in the middle of the dining room table. I didn't remember the house being this cramped, but everything was where it was meant to be. Nothing had changed. A painting that I'd executed as a high school student still hung on the wall by the dining room table. Calling the room a dining room was an insult to dining rooms. The room was far too small for something as luxurious as dining. No, we would eat there. Eating is far more pedestrian. Ordinary.

My father sat in his usual seat. My chair was still there. We, each of us—me, my mother, my father—occupied different styles of chairs. My chair was a reproduction of a Shaker chair. It was hard and wooden. My father's chair was a chrome number taken from behind a diner. My father thought the owner of the chair was throwing it out, but he was not. The chair was behind the diner because the owner of the diner liked to sit back there and smoke in between rushes. I knew this because I worked at the diner the summer of my fifteenth year, when my father was between jobs. "I don't smoke anymore," the owner said. His name was Supperclub Mike. No one knew why he was called Supperclub Mike. He was portly and seemingly covered over in a fine layer of yellow grease. Even his eyes, which bulged from his head and twitched side-to-side constantly, seemed to be covered in a fine layer of grease. "Some son of a bitch stole my smoking chair from out back." I looked around at all the chairs in the diner, and they all matched my father's chair. Same chrome. Same red vinyl. Same white vinyl. I gave Supperclub Mike a guilty look. "Do you know where my chair is? Do you? Do you, you little cunt?"

"No," I lied.

He didn't believe me. The rest of the summer, I spent cleaning out garbage cans. There were too many garbage cans in that little diner. They were all filthy. I wondered where they all came from.

I confronted my father about it and he said that Supperclub Mike shouldn't have left the chair outside if he didn't want someone—that someone being my father—to take the thing. "It was practically begging to be rescued. I couldn't let that chair sit out in the elements."

"Supperclub Mike can't smoke anymore because of you."

"Then I consider myself to be his savior," my father said. "You can see now that it was Christian of me." Another thing my father was proud of was rarely stepping foot in a church.

My mother listened to this exchange sitting in her own chair, a Danish modern number with an English racing green cloth seat, and said that my father was no savior. And also, that my father mumbled too much. "Blah, blah, blah, and nothing comes out," she said, sitting there in the floral housecoat she'd bought at a garage sale in 1994 from a woman who was packing up to move to Florida. She'd said to that woman, "What's in Florida that isn't in Ohio?"

"It's too cold here," the woman said.

"It's too something everywhere. But you'll find that out. Nothing but weirdoes down in Florida. And bugs." A thick cloud of mayflies drifted past and everyone standing in the driveway waved their hands in front of their faces.

"Lake Erie smells like chicken soup today," the woman said. It sounded like an accusation.

"That's the Cuyahoga River," my mother said.

"The Cuyahoga? We're not anywhere near the river."

"We're close enough."

"Do you want the housecoat or not?"

"I'll pay you a buck seventy-five for it."

"Fine."

My mother handed the woman two bucks. "You want the quarter back?"

"Of course I want the quarter back. Otherwise I would have said, 'two bucks.'"

The woman made a great show of slowly hiking back to the cash can she had on a card table near the garage. The garage was an attached garage, which my mother described as a "la-dee-dah attached garage. She can afford the quarter, selling a house with an attached garage. Fricking putting on airs like she is, with her fancy house."

My father had built the brick planter in front of the fancy house, so we knew how much money the woman had piled up in her coffers: Enough to build a fancy brick planter for her fancy house with a fancy attached garage. Now she was selling the place.

I think her name was Schmidt. Or maybe it was Schmelling.

The woman came back with the quarter and slapped it in my mother's palm like it was killing her to give it up. Who knows? Maybe it did. We heard a few months later that she'd died down in Florida. Something to do with the tides.

The painting up on the wall our eating room was of a platter of fruit. My mother liked the painting enough that she wanted it up on the wall. Or maybe she was being a supportive mother. I don't know. She'd had it framed properly.

"You got any syrup to go along with the waffles?" I asked, taking two plates out of the tiny cabinet above the miniature stove.

"These are savory waffles," my father said. "Not dessert waffles. If you're good, I'll make some dessert waffles next."

I looked down and saw a circular waffle iron on top of the stove. Next to it was a dog-eared copy of *Will It Waffle? A Guide to Waffle Cookery* by Lowell Thomas.

I set down the two plates and picked up the book. "Is this the same Lowell Thomas who—"

"No," my father said. "Hurry up with those plates. These waffles are fresh."

I brought the two plates over to our dining room table. Our eating table. The table in the nook where we consumed our food. I sat down and looked over at my mother's empty chair.

"Should we pray?" I asked.

"Pray? What would we want to do that for?" my father mumbled.

I heard him just fine, but out of habit, I said, "What?"

"God damn it. God damn it," he mumbled. Or something like that. He failed to enunciate. He often didn't. He glared at me and said, "Your mother isn't here. You know that. No praying anymore. We only eat waffles in this house. That's it. And no praying. I've mentioned that. It's okay that I repeat myself. Shut up. Shut up with your goddamn praying."

"Sorry," I went. I stabbed a waffle with my fork and it nearly fell apart as I dragged it to my plate. There were things inside it. Fish. Mashed potatoes. Maybe some sort of green vegetable. Mashed peas? My father had gone rogue in his waffle making. Lowell Thomas was to blame.

"Walleye," my father said, as I dissected the waffle with the tines of my fork. "Straight out of Lake Erie."

"Is it okay to—?"

"Of course it is! The EPA cleaned all that up decades ago. Are you crazy? Just eat your dinner. This is how dinner is done around here. Nothing out of the ordinary here. The waffle iron is a noble cooking device. It's been around for centuries in one form or another."

I ate the waffle without complaint, without thinking about the parts per picoliter that were probably composed of one toxin or other.

"We'll watch the Cavs later on. They'll win the NBA this year unless that Stephan Curry character steals it from us. Or the refs. The refs always have it in for Cleveland. Fucking refs." He muttered darkly for a while, none of which I could make out.

The waffles were missing something. Possibly, it was gluten. Some sort of unifying element. Something that would lend a chewing factor to the food.

My father finished, coughed into a paper napkin, and hauled himself wearily to his feet to shuffle back to the cooking implement of his choice to create a dessert. He mumbled something.

"What's that?" I asked.

"I said, 'chocolate chip waffles.' Would that warm your heart?"

"My heart?"

"I said it! You heard me. Your heart! You know that your mother called out your name while she was dying. Your only mother. Her only child. You couldn't be bothered to come back home for that. No. It takes your life falling apart for you to come back and visit your old, broken down dad. The neighbors all look in on me and wonder where the hell you are. They used to bring casseroles, but I guess that got old. I'm still here. Mostly. Mostly still here. Mostly functioning. Getting by on my Social Security checks. You'll have to find a job. When are you planning on looking for a job? I hope tomorrow. I can't support both of us on my Social Security checks. I'm a broken man. Your mother wouldn't forgive me if I let us both starve. Look at me while I'm talking to you. Look at your broken down old dad. Can't you even give me that courtesy? Jesus H. Christ. I'm a broken man. I haven't got anything but an ungrateful son who couldn't even be bothered to visit his dying mother when all she wanted was one last glimpse of her boy. Did you know that she prayed for you the entire time you were in Iraq? It was Iraq, wasn't it? Not Iran? We're not at war with Iran right now. I think that was in the nineteen eighties or so. Jimmy Carter. Helicopters and stuff."

"It was Iraq."

"Who can remember? Now do you like chocolate chips in your waffles? How about nuts? I have mixed salted nuts here. I could grind them up, maybe smash'm with a hammer. The hammer is in the basement near the water heater. Don't go down there! I have a project going on down there. You'll disturb it. Also, we're on the verge of needing a new water heater."

"I don't need nuts in my waffle."

"How about Hershey's syrup? You want some of that?"

"Only if we have some."

"Well, we don't."

"Then, no. I don't need Hershey's syrup."

"Your mother only needed to see you one last time, but you couldn't be bothered."

"I'm sorry."

"Sorry doesn't pay the bills."

"I don't know what else to say."

"I like a lot of chocolate chips in mine."

"Okay."

"That's just the way I like 'em. I don't know how they make chocolate chip waffles in Chicago. Those Illinois assholes."

"They make them with plenty of chocolate chips."

"Good. At least they do something right there."

"Do you need any help?"

"You think I can't make a waffle? I used to build walls. Sturdy walls. Walls that are still standing. That's a legacy, kiddo. I guess it don't create wealth like trading pork bellies in Chicago, but I guess I'll have to live with my leaving a physical legacy behind instead of filling other people's bank accounts with loot. Whipped topping? I got the real stuff, not the Cool Whip. Nothing wrong with Cool Whip. But this stuff's pretty good. Comes in a squirt can. Almost as good as ice cream. I'm out of ice cream, so don't ask."

"I'll take a squirt of whipped topping."

"There's a good lad. You're too skinny. You still drawing those stupid comics?"

"No. I gave it up after the Army."

"Too bad. You were pretty good at it."

"Thanks." I was good at the illustration work, but not making up my own stories. Instead, I'd draw episodes of *Star Trek* from memory.

"Physical legacy."

Steam rose out of the waffle iron as it cooked the dessert waffles. My father stood on shaky legs in the kitchen. His pants were stained with paint and mortar. His boots were worn and cracked. He wore a faded pocket t-shirt. His veiny hands shook. And the beard. It was like out of some sort of fever dream of bad beards. His longish hair was slicked back with Vitalis. Or sweat.

"I'm here now, dad. I'm here." I looked out the front window. The neighbors were out in the street, gathered around the smoldering remains of my car.

"It's too late," he said. "Too, too late."

MY FATHER'S DISPUTE WITH THE STATE OF OHIO

My father kicked the bed and jarred me awake from a dream in which I was playing catch on a sandy beach with Tim Couch. There was no ocean by this beach. No seagulls. Just me and Tim Couch. No sound. The sun was scorching. He soft-tossed the ball to me, just hard enough for me to catch it. A professional quarterback like Couch could have zipped the ball in and broken my sternum or busted my head, but not him. He was so very cool. During a break, we enjoyed classic orange-flavored Gatorades.

"Wake up, dummy!" my father shouted. I rolled over and looked at the Big Ben ticking on the nightstand. Six a.m.

"It's six a.m.," I mumbled. "I'm sore."

"You're sore, huh? I did most of the work." If by "most of the work" he meant that he leaned on his aluminum walker and shouted at me while I scooped up the remains of my once-treasured Mustang and placed them in five-gallon PVC buckets then, yes, he did most of the work.

The neighbors stood around in a semicircle and gawked during this. Some of them took pictures and videos with their phones and posted the resulting evidence to social media, where I was mocked as the goofball who set his car on fire and had to scoop it up with a spade while his father barked out instructions such as "put your back into it" and "get lower and slower, dummy."

"Dummy" is the charming nickname my father gave me when I was a child.

"You need a job, dummy," my father said.

"That's true. Is anyone hiring at six a.m.? Is there a donut shop around here that has management on site, ready to hire at a moment's notice?"

"Funny." Stone-faced. Staring. One eye was twitching under a tuft of hair that either came from his cowlick or cascaded from his eyebrow. And the twitching eye—was it a pre-stroke tic? For a moment, my father blurred, became indistinct. He came back into focus. He looked at his blurry hand and then looked at me. "Did you see that?"

"See what?" I wasn't going to give him the satisfaction.

"Never mind," he snarled. "Get your ass out of bed, dummy. We need to find you a job today."

"I don't know if you noticed, but I don't have a car."

"You can have mine."

"You don't own a car." The state of Ohio had taken it away after my mother died. They'd towed it away during the funeral, while we were all inside St. Sebastian's Catholic Church. It was a 1970 AMC Rambler station wagon that my father hadn't bothered to have inspected since, possibly, the mid-nineteen-eighties. The tags hadn't been renewed since the late-nineteen-nineties. My father's driver's license wasn't current either. He claimed to have a dispute with the state of Ohio. Ohio owed him. There was no way around it. He wasn't going to budge. For years he had the upper hand, but Ohio caught up with him during a moment of weakness. He'd shed a tear during the funeral, and Ohio towed his car. There was a direct correlation, according to my father. He drew a diagram on the living room wall with a piece of a child's crayon after the funeral. Like St. Sebastian, my father was clearly being made a martyr by The Man. The diagram proved it. Somewhere in the diagram was my father actually stepping foot into a church, which he believed violated some sort of pact he had with the Almighty. My wife pulled our daughter into her lap, sitting on the shabby sofa where my mother used to watch soap operas, her stories. My wife glared over at me. Clearly, my father was my fault. I finished off the bottle of Schlitz in my left hand and the mustard and pickle sandwich in my right. This was all somebody's fault, this whole wrong scene.

"I have something better than a car," my father said, grinning. "Wouldn't you like to know what that is?"

"Give me another hour of shuteye," I said.

"Don't give me that sour look. That's the same sour look that killed your mother. The same one you gave her right before you ran off."

"I didn't run off. You signed me into the Army. Remember that? You filled out the paperwork. You said it would turn me into a man, like the Ohio Air National Guard turned you into a man."

"The Army clearly wasn't as tough as I thought it would be. The military was tougher in my day." My father was an athletic equipment specialist in the Ohio Air National Guard. He worked in the gym at the Zanesville Air National Guard Base one weekend a month during the Ford, Carter and Reagan administrations, handing out basketballs and mopping up sweat from the racketball courts. Two weeks a year, usually during the fall so he could catch an Ohio State game, he'd go down to Rickenbacker Air National Guard Base in Columbus and hand out gym equipment there. "I see you giving me that look. I did my time. I served." He had a COLD WAR VETERAN ball cap to prove it. "You damn kids. You don't know what real sacrifice is like. Now get up. We have to go to the guild hall."

"The guild hall is in downtown Cleveland."

"No duh, dummy. We'll take the rapid's."

I dragged myself out of bed. My back spasmed. So did my jaw from all the clenching I'd done.

I took a long, cold shower and scrubbed myself down again. I still had black goo wriggling out of my pores and oozing from beneath my fingernails. After the shower, I opened my closet and found my jeans and t-shirts from high school in a cardboard box labeled "Phil's Crap." There was some threadbare underwear and socks in there, too. It all fit, strangely enough. I was an entirely different person now, shaped differently, but the clothes slid onto my body like they missed it. I sighed putting on those old clothes. I nearly hugged myself in them.

I ventured into the dining room expecting more waffles, but the old man hadn't bothered. He'd slid the waffle iron into a special carrying bag. "We'll be making breakfast for the fellas," he said. "They're all waiting on us down at the guild hall. We'll have leads on a lot of jobs if we're lucky. Expensive jobs. Shaker Heights. They love walls in Shaker Heights." He glared at me. "Hurry up, hurry up. Let's go. That train's gonna leave whether or not we're on it. It doesn't run as often out here."

We were at the far western edge of Cleveland, almost in Rocky River. We had the church to go to, and the tavern. And the Polish buffet.

Cleveland, in case you don't know it, has a world class symphony orchestra.

We got out the door, but it was slow-going, what with my father's infirmity on display, tromping down the street slowly, the clack of the aluminum walker hitting the uneven pavement. It was a stroll of sorts down memory lane. I waved to the few neighbors who hadn't come out to mock me. They were on their way to actual jobs. Every other yard had a sign on it announcing that the house was for sale. Some of them had signs announcing the date of an auction. We passed my high school sweetheart's house. Truth be told, she wasn't my high school sweetheart. I had a crush on her. It wasn't reciprocated. I walked around St. Sebastian's Catholic High School looking like someone had killed my dog. Truth be told, someone had killed my dog. I found him, a Jack Russell terrier who I'd named Omar (after Omar Vizquel), in a heap in my back yard. He shouldn't have been out of the house, but my mother's brother came over, drank half of the Carling Black Label in the fridge, and decided that he wanted to horse around outside with my dog. My mother begged him not to, but he told her that dogs need exercise and her little fairy son was not fit to be a dog owner, what with his artistic pretensions and all, so he, my uncle, would do the right thing and take the dog out front and possibly throw a stick for the little fucker so he could get some goddamned exercise. "Don't try to stop me, Marie!" he shouted, opened the door, and out went Omar into the street where a red Toyota ran him down. Or possibly it was a Honda, or maybe it was a Nissan. All that my uncle knew was that the fucking car was a red rice-burner that had cost him a job with the Ford assembly plant in Lorain, Ohio, and now the Japs had cost his beloved nephew his dog. He told my mother that he'd bury the dog out back, but instead he placed the dog in the middle of the yard for me to discover.

My uncle's name is Liam, in case you're wondering. He'll turn up later. He always does.

So I buried the dog. The girl I had a crush on, Patty McGinty, with her blond hair and pale skin, her blue-green eyes like the sea, stood on the other side of the fence atop a skateboard. I'd drawn her several times by then, with a couple renderings that were more speculative than based on real life. Those were underneath my mattress. I was filled with Catholic guilt about them. I'm still filled with Catholic guilt about them. "What happened to him? He was such a cute little dog. Energetic," she said. She had an adorable lisp, like Linus did in the animated *Peanuts* specials.

"My uncle happened to him. He's a drunk." I furiously dug the hole in the middle of the yard, right next to a white, cement birdbath with dark, fetid water bubbling like Diet Coke in the middle of it.

"Everyone's uncle is a drunk," she said. "That's no excuse for dog murder."

I was sweaty and dirty. This was my chance to tell her how I felt. I said, "I've had a crush on you since the eighth grade." I didn't look up, kept on digging, panting, sweating. My poor little dog lay dead on the ground between us. He was beginning to attract flies.

"Everyone has a crush on me. It's because I developed boobs first. Even some of the girls have crushes on me. You'll get over it at some point." She stepped off her skateboard, stomped on the back of it and caught it as it flipped into the air. "See you later, art boy." She walked off.

"Patty!" I shouted, dropping the shovel. I started to run to her, but tripped over my dead dog.

"You better get that dog in the ground. He's starting to stink," she said, without breaking stride.

I took her advice.

I stared at her house as my father and I walked past. I squinted at it like squinting would give me x-ray eyes.

"She doesn't live there anymore," my father said.

"Who doesn't?"

"That girl who you drew all the naked pictures of," he said too loudly.

"Right."

"I mean, goddamn boy, I thought you were queer until your mother waved those drawings in my face. Proudest moment of my life. My son is a man! Well... not queer anyway. And you managed to reproduce. What's the name of your daughter again?"

"Your granddaughter's name is Annie."

"Jesus H. Christ. What a boring name. No wonder I keep forgetting it."

"You need to take a rest, dad? We've walked half a block. Sure you don't need a salt pill?"

"Oh, ha, ha, ha, dummy. Making fun of your crippled father."

"You could jog if you wanted to. This is all in case some Social Security agent is hiding in the bushes."

"Shut your goddamned lying mouth, son."

"You could dance the Watusi if you wanted."

"I'm warning you, dummy. Shut your mouth." He glared around, like he suspected that some Social Security cop was in the bushes right then and there.

"You're only doing this because no one wants a brick wall anymore. This is your early retirement plan."

He peered around for a moment, saw no one, dropped the walker, strode over and smacked me in the back of the head. He walked back over and picked up the walker and we continued the slow trek to the rapid transit station in silence.

We made it there eventually.

The station had seen better times. I'm sure that when the station was erected in the post-war era, it was the pride of Kamm's Corners. Now, it was a mustard-colored wreck, with a mercury vapor lamp that was uncertain if it was night or day. The sky above was the color of a subtle nervous breakdown. There was a faint whiff of Chinese food in the air. A suspicious stain marred the concrete pad on which we stood. Bits of the pad crumbled off the edge and onto the tracks, which glowed like a radioactive 3D monster who was nearly ready to rise from the depths of a South American lagoon and maybe wrestle Johnny Weissmuller. The electrical line that powered the railcars hummed overhead. I held up my hand experimentally and the hairs on the back of it stood straight up.

"This line isn't supposed to run anymore, but it does. They forgot about it," my father said.

Ironically, this was probably due to my father's old enemies at the Ohio Department of Transportation—OhDOT.

We could hear the railcar rumbling far off before we saw it. The railcar looked like someone had haphazardly welded two city buses together. Sparks flew above it. It squealed to a halt in front of us and the double doors opened to reveal an empty shell. There were no seats. There were merely a few metal poles to hang onto. I helped my father in. He turned around the walker and managed to use it as a chair. The doors clapped shut. The railcar jerked forward and stopped. Then jerked forward again, and then stopped again. It began to chug forward. It slowly built up a head of steam. A kaleidoscope of sparks whirled around us, like we were in the midst of an electrical aura. Buh-bump, buh-bump, buh-bump. I peered through the yellowed and cracked windows, but could make nothing out but vague motion. Someone had left a life-size head of Mayor McCheese in the car. I sat down on it and it deflated to the chipped wooden floorboards.

"Could be rats under that thing," my father noted.

"Could be," I went. I rolled my eyes at the thought, but at the same time hoped he wasn't right.

"Where's the fucking waffle iron?" my father asked in a panic. He stood up and realized that he'd been sitting on it. He'd strapped the special waffle iron carrier to the walker. "Jesus H. Christ, that gave me a scare. We're cooking breakfast for the boys." Most of the boys, if memory served, would be in their seventies by now. Some would be in their eighties or nineties if they still lived. "First thing, we get your certifications in order. Then there's the part where they whack you with a stick."

"Right," I said. "The ancient, secret rites."

"Don't mock. And then we'll take a look at the jobs board. Plenty of jobs this time of year. It's building season. Rich people don't want to see the street. They want walls. Solid walls. Walls that are, um…"

"Opaque."

"Sure, throw around your five-dollar words."

"Just trying to be helpful. I imagine that you'll be on hand to supervise when I'm building these walls."

"I'm here to support you, son."

"Swell."

"Look, we can turn around this… right. We're not turning around. Let's get your certifications in order and get some work. Is that so much to ask? I'm sure your daughter, old whatshername, needs stuff for school, or some goddamned thing. Candy! Kids like candy. You did. I think. Anyway, she'll need things that her mother can't provide. Man things. Solid things."

"Tangible things."

"Right. Whatever."

I sifted through my memories, looking for an out. I found one. "I could go back to school. Get a degree. I've still got two years of my G.I. Bill money."

"You?!" my father went incredulously. "You? In school? You?"

"I have a business degree. An associate's degree," I said defensively.

The railcar lurched to a halt. A horn-shaped speaker lodged in the ceiling above my head spooled out some static followed by a feral scream followed by piercing feedback followed by a woman's calm voice that uttered one dismal word: "Delay."

"Shit." My father looked at his wrist, which had no watch on it.

I pulled my phone out of my pocket. No Service.

The railcar traveled backward for about thirty seconds. It stopped. The horn-shaped speaker squealed like a rusty nail dragged across a blackboard. The railcar lurched forward again and we continued our journey downtown. We dipped into a long, dark tunnel. The sparks above were more subdued. I could make out the outlines of faces and figures as we zipped through. I could hear a distant clang, like someone hit a metal rod with a metal hammer. We emerged into blinding sunlight, the sun was out, and we were high above the downtown, suspended in midair on a slight bridge. I wiped a nearby window clean with my handkerchief, leaving a circular, muddy smear, and peered down at the city in all its glory. This was the land of my birth. Five steel plants spewed out five towers of flame, the crooked river gushing past them. I blinked and we were at ground level again, somewhere on the near east side. The railcar came to a stop. The feminine voice crackled in the speaker above my head. I struggled to my feet. "Out," she said. "Out!" A long, low buzz filled the car. It became a scream. I slapped my hands over my ears and struggled to the door. The scream ended. Silence. Then came a whisper: "Thank you for riding your R.T.A."

"Don't mention it," said my father, clumping toward the door with his walker.

TEN CENT BEER NIGHT

We emerged from the downtown Rapid Transit station onto Ontario. Or maybe it was Lorain Avenue. Nothing looked familiar. The river smelled like iron filings and raw sweat. I tromped behind my father, trying to get my bearings. I gave up. "Where the hell are we, dad?"

"This is the new Cleveland. The better Cleveland. The one that our ancestors tried to build, succeeded in building, and we had stolen away from us. It's back. It's better. Wait til you see the Flats. They're better. And you can fish out of the river. No joke. There are fish in it. Walleye. Perch. Some sort of angry Chinese carp. They'll look right at you when you're fishing, those angry Chinese carp. They know the game's afoot. They're tough to catch. Sometimes they'll leap way up out of the water and head-butt you."

"I'm not eating a fish out of the river."

"No one asked you to, dummy."

I followed my father into a blind alley. At the other end of it, we found the new guild hall. "Wait, what happened to the old guild hall?"

"Oh, look who cares about the guild hall now. Hey, sometimes different is better. Sometimes better is better. This place is better than the old one."

"Didn't this used to be the Forest City Bakery?"

"They're in the old guild hall now. They needed an industrial crane to lift the ovens out of this place and put them on barges on the river. Then the cranes drove down to the old guild hall, which is now the bakery, and met the barges. They drove about two miles per hour. People went nuts. It was a great day—one of those banner days for Cleveland, I can tell you, like when Mayor Kucinich was voted out of office. Go dance a jig somewhere else, you socialist midget! Cleveland doesn't need you!"

I could hear the river flowing nearby. I could hear the sploosh-sploosh of what I assumed were angry Chinese carp flinging themselves out of the water, looking for fishermen to head-butt.

My father knocked on the door—a rapid three raps followed by two long hard knocks. A small door within the door slid open, revealing a grizzled face. The door slid shut. "It's Larry!" my father shouted. "Goddamn it, open the fucking door."

The door clanked open. It was made out of interlocking slabs of metal. A small ship's wheel, also metal, spun counterclockwise in the middle. Small panels clacked and snapped. With a loud metallic creak, the door slowly swung open, revealing the nearly empty guild hall. I followed my father in. The door shut with a loud clang behind us. Metal slats clacked back into place securing it.

"Wait," the old man who'd worked the door went. "Who's this?"

"It's Phil."

"Phil."

"My son. Phil."

"You have progeny."

"You've seen him before. I took him on jobs."

"I only watch jobs. I don't perform jobs. That's my function in the guild. We all have our function. Stones. Mortar. Lifting. Mixing. Astrolabe. Functions." The old man was getting worked up. We was dressed in a ceremonial robe. It was red satin and had a fierce-looking fire-breathing tiger or lion appliqué on the back of it. His name, Del, was stitched in cursive on the front. He wore a ceremonial hat composed of plaited copper wire atop his head.

My father dumped the walker on the cracked tile floor near the entrance, untied the waffle iron bag and slung it over his shoulder. "C'mon, dummy. We have waffles to make."

"Fine," I said.

"Is this the one you want me to hit with the rod of obedience?" Del asked.

"Not now. Later," my father said. He strode across an area that used to be covered over in ovens and bakers, but now had a dozen or so stone masons milling about. There were no chairs to sit on. The ceiling was coated in soot. A sweet-sour scent danced in the air. Men's voices echoed off the bare brick walls.

We got to one of the far walls, where a small generator awaited us. My father plugged in the waffle iron and set it on a folding table next to a foot-high stack of styrofoam plates. An industrial-sized ceramic jug of "Naturally Occurring Syrup from the Woods of Northern Canada" was next to the plates, along with a cardboard box of plastic utensils.

"What are we planning on putting in the waffle iron?" I asked my father.

"Look behind you," he said. On the wall, there were two spigots. Above each spigot was a sign covered over in soot. I wiped one sign with my dirty handkerchief: CREME FILLING. I wiped the other: SPONGE MIX. My father handed me a tin cup. "Fill it."

I filled the cup with a foamy batter from the SPONGE MIX spigot and handed it to my father, who poured it onto the now-heated griddle. He handed me another tin cup.

"What am I supposed to do with this?"

"Creme filling," he said.

"How can it be any good? Shouldn't it have gone bad by now?"

"It'll last a thousand years," he said. "The pipes are filled with it and they extend all over the city. Smart kids have been leeching creme filling for years from busted pipes. You should have seen it when they hit the one pipeline when they were tearing down old Municipal Stadium. A gusher of creme filling! And kids running around with their mouths open."

"I remember that." I'd seen it in the *Plain Dealer* the following day. It was a mob scene reminiscent of Ten Cent Beer Night, the game when the Cleveland Indians decided that they wanted to fill up Municipal Stadium, an eighty-thousand-seat wreck that was encircled by pesky seagulls and always four-fifths empty when the Indians were in town. The Indians decided to sell beer for ten cents a cup, and suddenly the place was packed. This was the mid-nineteen-seventies, an era when the Indians were consistently awful. Over 80,000 drunk Clevelanders lost their drunken minds, especially after seeing the hated Billy Martin, a contemptible Yankee disguised as a Texas Ranger, taunting them in the opposing dugout. He danced and pulled his pants down and slapped his bare ass. He thumbed his nose in a way that made the drunks remember decades of humiliation at the hands of the hated Yankees. My father's Ohio Air National

Guard unit was called up to put down the riots that lasted three days and three nights. Billy Martin was tied up and taken hostage, eventually spirited away to the spire atop Terminal Tower. The massive Chief Wahoo effigy atop the stadium was taken down and paraded through the near east side and near west side, eventually coming to rest next to a home for retired postal workers. The Indians finally sold out of all their beer on the third day, and the drunks sobered up and ambled home to their spouses and children, feeling only slightly ashamed of themselves. Billy Martin was returned unharmed in a soggy cardboard box via Parcel Post to the Yankees. This was ten years before I was born, but I learned all about it in my Problems With Contemporary Society class at St. Sebastian High. Our teacher, Father Bob, a priest who'd taken his holy orders at Notre Dame —the famous one in Indiana, not the one in Elyria—told us with no small amount of pride how he'd helped his father duct-tape Billy Martin to a hand-painted mural of Bob Feller made of rusty bottle caps and pull-tops from Carling Black Label bottles and cans. "Take that you dirty Yankee!" the priest recalled his father saying before placing a strip of duct tape over Billy Martin's filthy Yankee mouth and punching him in his dirty Yankee guts. They left him there, high above the city, adhesed to Terminal Tower, crying his bitter Yankee tears. All of this was memorialized in a Lite Beer commercial that ended with Boog Powell wandering onto the set, putting on a pair of Coke bottle glasses, looking into a mirror and declaring, "I'm Boog Powell."

My father finished up the first of a couple dozen waffles made of sponge cake batter and placed them on a styrofoam plate. Our first customer waddled up, an overstuffed septuagenerian with a name tag that announced him as a Grand and Ancient Degreed Seminarian. "Creme?" I asked him.

"Pretty please," he said.

I held the plate underneath the CREME FILLING spigot and it oozed out a fluffy blob of sugary white goo.

The Grand and Ancient Degreed Seminarian held the plate up to his bulbous nose, took a long and loving sniff, and said, "My." He snatched up a full set of plastic cutlery and walked away.

In the corner of the room farthest from us, deep in a shadow, I saw the glint of a man in a golden tuxedo. He walked up to a small Wurlitzer electric piano, sat down, hit the rumba key, and played, off in the distance, "The Girl from Ipanema." From what I could hear, it was a jaunty version of the classic song.

All the time we were cranking out waffles, the man played on and on. He dipped into some Nirvana at one point, and then into the catalog of Herb Alpert. He made all of the songs, no matter the source material, sound zippy.

"That guy builds walls?" I asked my father.

"Yeah. What of it? You think that all we do is build walls? Some of us have hobbies. Side gigs."

"No need to get your tail up in the air," I said.

"What's that supposed to mean?"

"I don't know."

"We're almost done." My father buzzed like static electricity for a moment and disappeared. The spatula he'd been holding clacked onto the table. A moment later, I heard another static buzz and he reappeared. "Don't tell me you didn't see that."

"I saw it."

"What do you make of it?"

"I don't know."

"Jesus H. Christ, you're just about useless." He made two more waffles. He handed me one, and took the other for himself. "Put the creme on it. Trust me."

I put creme on each of our waffles. He wasn't wrong. I took one bite and was nearly transported to another world myself. At least that's what I assumed happened when my father disappeared. I didn't want to ask him. It seemed like too personal a question.

One of the old timers shambled up and placed his plate on the table. He'd licked it clean. "I know you," he said, wagging a bent index finger under my nose.

"I'm Phil. His son."

"I thought you left!" It was as much an accusation as an observation.

"I did leave."

"Now you're back. Couldn't stay away, huh?"

"I guess not."

"Not such a big shot now, are you?"

"I guess not."

He seemed satisfied. "So you want to be a stone mason, huh?"

"I already am, according to my father."

"There's only one small rite we have to perform. Isn't that right, Larry?"

"Yes," my father said. "Just the one."

"Del!" the man shouted over his shoulder. "Get on over here. It's time!"

Del walked over in his ridiculous robe, brandishing a wooden stick that looked more like a mop handle than some sort of ritual totem.

The old man said, "Do you accept the rules and regulations of the guild as pertaining to… something, something. You get the idea. Say 'yes.'"

"Yes," I said.

Del, a surprisingly spry old man, vaulted over the folding table and, in one motion, swung the rod of correction directly at the back of my left knee, dropping me to the floor. I rolled over onto my back. He stood over me smiling. "You gonna cry?"

"Maybe," I said.

"Well, don't," Del said. "Elsewise, I'll have to do it again. And harder."

The pain was intense. It seemed to well up in the back of the knee and suddenly shoot out to my entire body as a massive wave. A few moments later, the pain had passed.

My father helped me to my feet. "Good job."

"Is that it?" I asked.

"You wanna get hit again?" Del asked.

"No," I said.

"Okay then. That's it."

My father lifted three fingers—index, middle and ring—up to his right eyebrow. He bowed ever so slightly. Then everyone else made the same gesture. So I repeated the gesture. That seemed to finish the cycle.

The man who'd been playing the Wurlitzer stopped. A few moments later he was beside me in his gold satin tux. He had elaborate facial hair. There were braids and beads in it. He handed me a card: Buddy Riccardo and his International Band. See Us Live! He handed out a few more cards, shook some hands, and was on his way.

"What's on the job board, boys?" my father asked.

"Slim pickings," Del said. "But the good news is that none of us are in shape enough to build doodly squat."

"I suspected as much," my father said. He smiled and rubbed his hands together like a miser with a pile of gold in front of him. "Let's take a look!"

We walked over to the board, which was near the front door. There was one job on it, and as luck would have it, it was in Kamm's Corners, about two blocks from our house.

"Aren't you going to introduce me to your son?" the old man who'd licked his plate clean asked. He'd appeared suddenly behind us.

"Son, this is Ohio's Deputy Undersecretary of Transportation Merle Chestnut, the Grand Magnificent Leader of the stone mason guild. Merle is also the closest thing I have to an archenemy."

"We're not caped superheroes," Merle Chestnut said.

"Not even close," my father said.

"Need a ride home?" Merle Chestnut asked us.

"We'd appreciate it," I said.

"Come with me," he said, and then released a hideous laugh from deep inside his withered old body.

The door went through its metallic contortions and opened. Out front, on the curb, we were greeted by a familiar sight. It was my father's 1970 AMC Rambler station wagon, fully restored and gleaming with carnauba wax. A chauffeur in full black livery stood at attention, ready to drive the Deputy Undersecretary in our old car.

"I knew it," my father muttered almost inaudibly. "Knew it."

"Life's a kick in the pants, isn't it?" Merle Chestnut said. "Don't forget to pay your annual dues. After the job's done, of course."

My father gathered up all his stuff—his waffle iron and its carrier, his aluminum walker, my work assignment. He carried it all in his arms like a man with no secrets. I kept an eye on him. He could blink out of existence at any moment. We'd need to see a doctor about it.

The driver opened the back door to our old car and then the two of us performed a little dance, getting out of each other's way.

"Ope," I went.

"Ope," he went.

We both went "ope" one more time, and then I was butt-sliding across the back bench seat.

My father stuffed his crap in the back of the vehicle and then slid in next to me, sitting on the hump momentarily like a middle child. He slid over to the driver's side a moment later when he realized that the Deputy Undersecretary of Transportation was going to sit shotgun.

"Where we headed?" the driver asked.

"Home," my father said.

"And where is that?" he asked testily.

I gave him the address and he typed it into his phone, which was mounted on the dashboard next to a vent.

"Name's Bram," the driver said.

"I'm Phil and this is Larry," I said.

"And I'm Deputy Undersecretary of Transportation Merle Chestnut. Let's go."

Merle and my father sat glaring at it each other. Merle was going to get a crick in his neck if he kept it up.

"So what's your beef with each other?" I finally asked, a few miles down the road.

"It's professional," my father said.

"It's not that professional," Merle said.

They went back to their silence. It was uncomfortable, despite the air conditioner going full blast.

"So. Bram. Like Bram Stoker."

"Who's Bram Stocker?"

"Stoker. The writer."

"So what?"

"Pardon?"

"So what? What about Bram Stoker the writer?"

"I assume you're named after him."

"Maybe. What's he write?"

"He wrote *Dracula*. The original."

"You into that shit?"

"No."

"Then why you bring it up? Ain't nobody care about no Dracula shit. Am I right, pops?"

My father glanced up into the rearview mirror. "Why are you dragging me into this?"

"I'm just saying. Nobody's into no vampire shit. Leastways you. Am I right?"

"I have no idea what you two are going on about," my father said. He looked over at me. "It's a professional beef."

"Professional my ass," Bram said. "Ain't nothing professional about no vampire book. Shit. I'm just about done talking to your ass." He made a sudden turn onto the expressway and we all jerked from one side to the other.

"I am the master of the astrolabe," Merle Chestnut said. He'd crossed his arms and was staring straight ahead.

"Okay," I said.

"My calculations are not to be questioned."

"Here we go," my father said.

Merle turned around in his seat and glared at him. "To the micrometer, that's how I measure."

"You were off," my father said. "Everyone knows you were off. And the dogs. You know what I'm saying."

"The stars do not lie about borders. And sacrifices must be made."

"Wrong-o."

"And who has paid the price?" Merle asked, turning back around.

"Y'all need to kiss and make up or some shit," Bram said.

"This is my car! My car! And you've turned it into some sort of... I don't know. But it isn't serving its God-given purpose anymore. Who heard ever of an AMC Rambler being a limo? No one. That's who."

"It looks pretty nice. Smells nice, too," I said.

"Who asked you?" my father roared.

"It's a sleek driving machine now. Tuned to the stars," Merle said. "The stars reveal all to those who can read them."

"Motherfucking bullshit," Bram said.

His phone said, "Bram, pay attention or you're going to miss your exit."

"Yes, ma'am," Bram replied.

"We're coming up on it. Are you ready?" the phone said.

"Yes, ma'am."

"Here it comes. Are you sure you're ready?"

"Damn, woman!"

"Now!"

He swerved the car off the expressway. The old suspension rocked us back and forth, and we barreled down the ramp at an unsafe speed.

"Mmm. Here comes a light," the phone said. "Don't let the man catch you running a light."

"The man is sitting right next to you," my father said.

"Shut your damn mouth," Bram said. "Ain't nobody talk to my woman that way."

"It's just up here. Next light," I said.

"He's right," the phone said. "Turn here, baby."

After a few hundred yards, Bram pulled the car into our driveway, hopped out and held the door for me and my father. My father slowly made his way to the back of the vehicle. I got out, walked around and dropped the tailgate. I took the waffle iron and instructions for my job. My father removed his aluminum walker.

"It smells like someone lit a fucking car on fire around here," Bram said.

"Yeah. It was him," my father said, jerking a thumb in my direction.

"What you do that for?"

"I don't know," I said, shrugging. "Thanks for the ride."

"Thank him," Bram said, nodding toward the passenger seat.

I leaned over and thanked Merle.

"Think nothing of it. I will send you my readings for the job. I'm sure you'll do a better job interpreting them than your father ever did."

"Fuck you, mister undersecretary of my ass." My father clumped toward the house unspeedily. Our old station wagon backed out of our driveway and sped away. I watched it go. "That guy? That driver? He was white, right?"

"He was white."

"Then why'd he sound like that?"

"Like what?" He sounded like most of the people I'd served with in the Army.

"Jesus H. Christ, never mind." He muttered darkly for a moment. I think most of it was swearing.

"Should I call the number on this flyer today? Should I go over and size up the job? What should I take with me?"

"You should come inside and watch TV with me. I think the Indians are on this afternoon. Day game."

"But what about the job?"

"The job is an insult."

"But I'm still doing it, right?"

"Sure. But you need to find a real job. Something that pays. I know that address. I've built there before."

"Okay."

"It's not going to work out. But if you do a good job, maybe it will show people."

"Show people?"

"That they should have masonry work done. It's a noble profession. It builds nobility wherever it leaves behind a wall."

"Okay."

"In the meantime, I suggest you get on that phone of yours and find something that pays." He hobbled up the steps and went inside. I stood there in the driveway, confused.

"What're you doing out there, dummy?" he shouted through the window. "Bring that waffle iron inside! It's almost time for lunch."

I sat down on the driveway and looked up into the semi-hazy sky. I set the waffle iron down next to me. I pulled my phone out and scrolled through the ten or so names in my phone list. I poked on my ex-wife's name and the phone rang and rang. Finally, it went to voice mail. "Claire? Are you there? I need to talk to Annie. I'm looking for work. I swear I'll send money as soon as I can. I swear I'm not as bad a person as you say that I think I am." I looked around for a minute. The trees were coming around pretty nicely this spring, I thought. The grass was mostly green. The backyard looked pretty nice. I sat there for a while and stared at the birdbath and try not to think about my dead dog three feet below it. "I'm living with my father. You remember him from the funeral." What else was there to say? "I haven't had my pills in over twenty-four hours. They burned up in my car. Funny story. My car burned up. My Army uniforms are gone. So, see, I can part with my uniforms. I can get rid of them. I did get rid of them in a big old fire. And clearly I don't need my pills anymore. They weren't doing much good anyway. So, just so you know, I love you. My heart is broken. I miss you, Claire. I miss my poor dead mother. I miss my daughter." I thought about Annie for a moment, playing inside our apartment in Highland Park, running in circles inside, so full of energy. I couldn't let her go outside. That would ruin her energy, which came from a pure place. I remembered tumbling, once, out of a deuce-and-a-half and my head hitting the sand with a sickening thump. There were flames everywhere. Eventually, there was a guy named Doc whose face hovered over mine. He said, "That was cool!" Where was that? What country was that in? It was the scent of my destroyed Mustang dragging that memory out of me. That was what the pills were for, and all the visits to the VA, keeping those memories stored somewhere that was not in the present. The pills made it so things didn't replay in my mind over and over with my heart racing and racing like it wanted to leap out of my chest and make a break for it. I stared at the phone. What was it doing in my hand?

My father shouted out the window, "What're you doing out there, dummy? Feeling sorry for yourself? You should have thought about that before you fucked up your life. Get inside with that waffle iron. Pronto."

"Anyway. Goodbye," I said into the phone, and hung up.

I went inside and handed the bag containing the waffle iron to my father. The old tube TV set was warming up, making its peculiar sound that was somewhere between a note played on a cello and the tone coming out of an unattended Theremin. It would stop, I knew, the moment it was warm. It did so. Ronald Reagan was onscreen, wearing a cowboy hat. He smiled and said, "A man can take about anything, except being made a bigger fool than he already is."

"What happened to the ballgame?" I asked my father.

"Rain, or something."

"Rain?"

"Yeah, dummy. Rain. It rains sometimes. Look it up."

"When are you going to take this old Quasar to the dump?"

"When it stops working," my father said.

During a commercial break, Don Drake, who'd been the anchor for Action News Five since I was seven, came on to tease the evening news. "Coming up tonight at eleven… is the Toxic Blob in Lake Erie alive? Can it think? Can it speak? A professor from the Ohio State University thinks… yes! She says that that the Toxic Blob wants to… come home! More tonight at eleven on… Action News Five!" A graphic showed the Toxic Blob's progress toward the city's water intake pipe. Someone at the station's graphics department had drawn a smiley face on it. The Toxic Blob was the remains of what was scraped out of the river downtown after it caught fire. We thought it had been buried in the bottom of Lake Erie, and it had been, but now it was coming back to Cleveland, forty-five years later.

I could smell whatever waffles my father was cooking up. "Is that Ranch dressing?" I asked.

"It's a surprise. You find a job yet?"

I shifted on our ratty couch and opened up the Jobster app. "Gotta update my address," I said. I poked around in the app and did so. A pop-up that I almost dismissed cheered for me. Balloons inflated and burst into sparkles.

"CONGRATULATIONS VETERAN! YOU'RE HIRED!" it announced.

I scrolled down. I'd been hired as a team member at Buy and Bye in the Heartland Mall in North Olmsted, only eight-point-one miles away, according the app. I'd start that night with the weekly New Employee Verification and Indoctrination Day, from closing time at eleven p.m. until opening time at seven a.m.

"You get a job yet?" my father shouted from the other room. I could smell burning bacon now in addition to boiling Ranch dressing.

"Yes. But I need a car," I said.

"I've got something better," my father said. "I'll show it to you after lunch."

MADE IN PERU

My father had a spare toothbrush, and I made great use of it after lunch attempting to scrub his latest batch of waffles from my mouth. I resolved to somehow take over the cooking. After brushing failed to remove the aftertaste, I dug through his medicine cabinet and found something called "Konrath's Kure." It was green, and therefore, in my mind, minty. I figured I could swish it around a bit and maybe get rid of the foul bacon-ranch waffle aftertaste that way. I swished for a while and then swallowed, figuring what the hell. Maybe I can sleep through the aftertaste. I felt a bit dizzy after swallowing, so I read the label. The first ingredient was dextromethorphan HBr. The second was trichloromethane. The third was camphor. Then there were various numbered dyes. "Developed by a crack team at the Elkhart Institute," said the label. The ailments it claimed to "Kure" included "boils, infestation of lice in the nether regions, pleurisy, old maid's knee and colds due to damp weather and the like." No real warnings on the label to speak of. "To be taken either topically or internally, depending on the ailment." My father also had a dozen amber vials of pills from various Mexican pharmacies.

After I put the bottle away, I wandered around our tiny house, looking for my father.

The Konrath's Kure made me feel both loopy and slightly more focused than usual. I remembered that my father had told me not to go down into the basement. So I went into the basement. "Yoo-hoo!" I called, half-stumbling down the wooden staircase. The hot water heater ticked ominously in the corner. When I refused to finish my mush as a child, my father would force me to go down into the dark depths and sit next to that same water heater. It had seemed much larger back then—both the basement and the water heater. Time tends to shrink things. I wasn't allowed out of the basement until I stopped "wasting food." Like giving me twice as much oatmeal as I could possibly eat in one sitting wasn't wasting food. My father thought I was too skinny. Also, he thought my interest in art was going to make me gay. The basement would cure the gay. The fact that I didn't end up being gay, he told anyone who'd listen, was proof that the basement treatment worked. "Ipso facto faggo," he said to Johnny the Mailman within earshot of me. I found two sawhorses down in the basement and a piece of wood, a two-by-six board, laid across them. A handsaw was nearby. A broom and a dustpan stood ready to clean up should my father decide to saw the two-by-six in half. I found a carpenter's pencil, unsharpened, and a tape measure on the bare cement floor. I checked the washer and there were clothes in there that had stiffened and dried after a long ago rinse cycle. I shut the washer and made a mental note of it. There were a dozen stiff socks in the dryer. I climbed the stairs out of the basement and went outside. I squinted up at the too-bright sun.

I found my father behind our detached garage, at the far southern edge of our tiny lot, attempting to get a motorcycle started. "It won't turn over," he said. A radio inside the garage was playing:

Here comes D.J. Disco Tex
Truckin' with his Sex-O-Lettes
Get dancing, dancing, dancing!

"I thought you were against disco from way back," I said. "Didn't you go to Chicago to participate in Disco Demolition Day?"

It was one of the few times my father ever left the state of Ohio, other than his forays to Mexico to visit pharmacies there. He traveled to a Chicago White Sox game to watch disco records burn. A man bumped into him at Comiskey Park and the two of them got into a fight because my father was certain that the man had stolen his wallet. My father had forgotten that he'd placed his wallet in his front pocket in anticipation of being in a crime-ridden hellhole like Chicago. My father's perception may have been colored by the number of beers he'd consumed in anticipation of watching a Chicago DJ dynamite a truckload of disco records somewhere in the vicinity of center field. The two men were arrested for causing a public disturbance at Disco Demolition Night and hauled off to the jail inside the ballpark, a dank cellar that had once held Charlie Comiskey's private stash of Canadian whiskey during Prohibition. After my father

explained how the man had thieved from him, the cop made him
turn out his pockets and discovered my father's wallet along with
his out-of-state driver's license and his pink Ohio Air National
Guard ID card. "What's dis?" the cop said, waving the wallet and
ID cards around. He threw the wallet and cards at my father and
then carefully took out his baton and hit him with it three times.
Maybe four. He replaced the baton. "Get da hell out of here and
never come back to Chicago, you bum." My father took that to
mean: Never again leave Ohio. He told this story to anyone who
contemplated leaving Ohio, as if the rest of the world was a
treacherous place filled with angry Chicago cops. Other than
pharmaceutical trips on a red eye to Mexico, my father rarely left
Ohio.

"Who can remember what happened decades ago?"

"You tell that story all the time."

"Tell what story? Look, this is the only station that comes in
on that radio. You get used to it. Why don't you see if you can get
this motorcycle running?"

We traded places and now I was atop the aged motorcycle. I
unscrewed the chrome lid on the gas tank and discovered the
problem. I looked at my father expectantly.

"Fine," he snapped. He hobbled around the garage and came
back with the gas can for the lawn mower.

I swished the gas around in it to make sure that it hadn't
turned into varnish and then filled the tiny tank. I handed the
gas can back to my father and screwed the lid back on the gas
tank. I pulled the throttle a bit and kicked it over. Black smoke
poured out of the single exhaust pipe. I guided the motorcycle
out of its haven behind the garage and into the driveway. My
father went into the garage and produced an orange helmet. The
motorcycle backfired and the weeds growing through the cracks
in the driveway behind me caught fire.

"Fuerte!" my father shouted above the din.

"What's that dad?"

"Fuerte! That's the motorcycle brand. (Inaudible.)"

"What's that dad?"

"I said, 'It comes from Peru!'" He spun his finger around like
he wanted me to take it on a spin.

I put the helmet on and secured the chin strap. I lowered the yellowed and cracked visor. It was crusted over in long-dead mayflies. I pulled out of our driveway, slid a bit in the oily remains of my burned up car, and headed down Valleyview Avenue toward the tavern.

Ziska's Tavern was, miraculously, still open. Still in business. Still standing. It was next door to where I went to elementary school, which had been renamed three times since I'd gone there. Once, it was renamed after a city councilman who'd subsequently had been locked up for enriching himself and his family out of the public coffers. The second time, it was renamed after Johnny Manziel, the star quarterback for the Cleveland Browns who'd subsequently gone on a booze and cocaine bender and lost his job. The third time it was given back its original name, Valleyview Elementary, because sometimes you should leave well enough alone.

I parked out front and left the helmet on top of the seat. I went inside the tavern. Old Joe Ziska was standing there, wiping a glass. I could barely see him through the dim lighting. One of the old regulars was sitting at the bar, Frank Novak. A massive jar of pickled eggs, possibly the same one from when I was a kid, sat on the bar. This is what I came for.

"Joe," I said.

"Hey, Frank," Joe said, shaking Frank awake. "Look! It's Larry Derleth's kid. Wake up!"

"What?" Frank went. He lifted his head from the bar and glared at me. A peanut husk was stuck to his cheek. "Pfft. Check his ID."

"He's back from the war."

"War? What war?"

"You know. The war. Overseas. The one on TV."

"Pfft. Some war."

"It's a war. Show some respect."

Frank laid his head back down. "Pfft."

Joe shook him some more. "No sleeping at the bar."

Frank sat up and blinked at him. "Since when?"

"Since now."

"You're gonna lose a lot of business treating your customers this way."

"Uh huh."

I unscrewed the big jar and reached in. I pulled out a good one. Pungent. "Pull me a Black Label, will you Joe?"

"Sure," Joe said. He took the glass he'd been wiping down over to a spigot and pulled me a beer. I slapped a five on the counter and Joe slid it back to me. "Your money's no good here, soldier boy."

"I've been out of the Army for years," I said.

"In that case…" Joe took the cash and stuck it in his shirt pocket.

I gnawed on the egg and it killed the taste of the waffle right away. I quickly washed it down with the beer. "Good seeing you."

"Leaving so soon?" Joe asked. "How's your old man?"

"Fair to middling," I said.

"Sorry about your mom."

"Me too."

"You back for good?"

"I'll see you around, Joe." I walked toward the door.

"Don't be a stranger!" Joe yelled after me.

I got back on the motorcycle, helmet unsecured, and weaved back home. I got off the motorcycle after I parked it on the charred weeds on the driveway. I inspected it. The lights all worked. Check. There was a current plate on the back. Check. The tires were both bald. Check. Black oil was seeping out of the crankcase. Check.

My phone rang. Unknown Number. I answered it. An automated voice said, "Hello Team Member! Don't forget that tonight is your first night of work! Don't forget to bring your important documents with you, including your D-D-Two-Fourteen! Your safety is important to us, so we'll need you to wear shoes that have soles firmly attached to them. You will also need to wear trousers that you can pull up to your waist and that extend to your ankles. You will also need to wear a shirt. Please respect your fellow Team Members and don't forget to wash and use the deodorant of your choice. Thank you for choosing to work at Buy and Bye. If you would like to hear this message again, press star-zero. If you understand and accept this message, press pound now." I pressed pound. "Super! See you tonight at eleven pee-em at your hometown Buy and Bye. Goodbye." The phone beeped three times and died. I must have forgotten to charge it. What if Claire called? Annie? I ran inside and found my father watching *Death Valley Days* on our old tube TV. "Dad? Do you have a charger?"

"You know that I'm an AMC man. I'd never own a Dodge."

"A phone charger."

"My phone is in the kitchen."

"My phone charger burned up with the car."

"Boo hoo. You goddamned kids are too attached to your phones. We didn't need to stare into phones in my day. We had TV."

"I'm going to take a ride down to that mall in North Olmsted."

"Let me know how that turns out."

"Sure."

"I'm kidding about that. I don't care."

"Maybe I'll just stay there until work starts tonight."

"But what about dinner?"

"I'll get something while I'm out."

"I've got a new batter that I'm trying out. It's runny."

"They've got a food court. I hope."

"All right then. See you later, dummy."

I went in my bedroom and fished through the drawers of my bureau. I found my DD-214 under a pile of socks and a citation for my Purple Heart. I took both and shoved them in an old St. Sebastian's High backpack. There were still a couple of papers in there that I'd written as a teenager. One of them was titled, "The Reasons Why a Good Catholic Boy Should Take Holy Orders." Another one was titled, "Martin Luther Remains a Dangerous Heretic." A third paper was a note that I'd written for Patty McGinty. I'd drawn a nice rendering of her in graphite on college-ruled paper. I wrote, "I like you, do you like me?" The answer was an emphatic, and repeatedly underlined, "NO!!!"

Message received. I made a point of steering clear of her from then on—a tough job to do in a school with three hundred

Catholics who all lived within the same five-block area. But I learned to dodge her. My strategy for avoiding Patty McGinty took me to the point of convincing my father that I should be allowed to join the Army at the tender age of seventeen. I didn't tell him that it was a tactic to avoid the possibility of seeing, or being in the vicinity of, Patty McGinty. The weight of my embarrassment at my own behavior was crushing me.

Upon learning of my patriotic intent, St. Sebastian's allowed me to take extra classes, graduate early, and then I left for basic combat training at Fort Jackson, South Carolina. My follow-on training for Multimedia Illustrator, MOS Twenty-Five-Mike, was at Fort Meade, Maryland. That's where the Army taught me their methods for art, and how to make PowerPoint presentations. All of us in the class were assured by our instructors that we had nothing to fear about the war, even though it was on TV constantly and looked like it was going badly. President Bush was on TV, wrestling words to the ground and throttling them. We'd all be sent to General Staffs, we were assured, where we would prepare PowerPoint presentations that would be presented to other General Staffs. Occasionally, we might be called upon to draw something—maybe a general's dog, or the general himself. I felt good about my prospects right up until I got orders to Headquarters and Headquarters Company, Twenty-Eighth Light Infantry Brigade at Forward Operating Base Eagle in southeastern Iraq.

"We're shit out of soldiers," SGT Crabby told me. He was my NCOIC. We called him "Crabby" either from his general attitude or the creatures who infested his genital region. SGT Crabby was from Chicago, and had a plan to get himself orders to Fort Sheridan, a leafy post north of Chicago, away from the hustle and bustle of city life and nearly a million miles from Iraq, give or take.

SGT Crabby had the armory assign me a rusted-out M16A2 rifle. The parts of the rifle that weren't rusted were composed of plastic that was falling apart bit-by-bit. Others in my ad hoc squad used the much smaller M4. We were given odd jobs to do that didn't require actual soldiering, we were assured by the second lieutenant in charge of our platoon, a squirrelly pimpled man barely out of adolescence like the rest of us. His favorite phrase was, "What're you asking me for? Ask Sergeant Crabby!" and then he'd hide from us inside the tiny shipping container that he shared with another second lieutenant from our company. I told him I was an illustrator, a proud Twenty-Five-Mike. "So what? That guy's in the Navy! He's not complaining!" The guy who he pointed toward was a Navy logistics specialist who'd somehow been reassigned to the Army off of a ship that was now sailing in the Mediterranean, visiting Monte Carlo and other ports of call. Everyone called him "Squid" in lieu of an actual name. My made-up name was "CC," short for "Combat Cartoonist." We bonded over burning shit.

There were others.

There was PFC Tanaka, a seventy-one lima, who never took off her battle rattle, even when burning shit. She wore her kevlar helmet, goggles, body armor, elbow and knee pads… everything, all the time. She wore it in her sleep.

There was PVT Brink, a forty-two romeo, an Army band baritone player, who always managed to be somewhere else whenever work was being performed, especially when that work involved burning shit. He was a tubby little man who enjoyed the MRE fruitcake. He hoarded them in a secret stash and was never without one to nibble on.

There was SPC Moonvie, an eleven mike, who tried to join the Navy, but was too tall. He walked in a way that suggested that he was not comfortable with his height. Someone nicknamed him "Beanpole," but it didn't stick. He was not a competent basketball player, which upset Crabby to no end. "What am I supposed to do with you, Moonvie?" he'd ask him. "This squad needs to win at something. We keep losing."

"I don't think that my weapon would fire if anything happened," I told Squid.

Squid said, "Don't think about it. Think about Naples, where my ship is homeported. Think about the blue Adriatic Sea." He said that he'd prefer to be called by his proper Navy name, which was "El-Ess-Three." It sounded complicated to our Army ears, so we kept on calling him "Squid."

Squid said that he'd had worse food than what was served in our dee-fac. He talked about a cruise where he ate spaghetti that was topped with ketchup. He said that there were worse things than being behind the wire in a forward operating base in the middle of the desert.

SGT Crabby asked him to list these worse things.

"Number one," Squid said, "is being on the other side of the wire." He pointed. "Over there."

"Point taken," SGT Crabby said. We stood and watched the shit burn and burn.

Another member of our little squad was Doc, a.k.a. John Wayne. John Wayne was two-thirds of his real name. The last third was on his uniform: BOSTICK. John Wayne was a medic. In addition to the burning shit in front of us, there was the actual shit that he'd seen out in the 'Stan. "Now that's a fucking war, my friend. That's a war you can hang your hat on. The 'Stan is for realsies. Lots of pow-pow and ouchie-ouchie and help! I need a medic! And: Oh my fucking God my fucking dick's been shot off!" Doc/John Wayne did a little pantomime of blood spurting out of a crotch wound. "It was all so glorious." Doc smiled at the memory of all the pow-pows and ouchie-ouchies he'd seen in the 'Stan. "Here, it's just a bunch of burning shit. I need action, Jackson. We should volunteer for convoy duty."

"Fuck no," SGT Crabby said. "And if I hear you volunteered us, I will go pow-wow and ouchie-ouchie all over your stupid ass."

"I take that as a challenge," Doc said.

"You best not, G.I. You best get your noggin right," SGT Crabby said.

"My noggin has a metal plate in it. I get great reception. I'm listening to WMMS in Cleveland right now. Rock and Roll Hootchie Koo, motherfucker."

"Oh, hey. You're from Cleveland? I'm from Cleveland, too."

"East side or west side?"

"West side."

"That's too bad. Too bad for you. Fuck-tard westsider. No one likes you."

"True enough," I said. I poured more kerosene on the flaming bucket of turds.

"Hey! Hey, dummy! What're you doing?" My father stood in next to my bed, his fists on his hips, his scraggly hair whirling around his head like a hobo's halo. A bit of waffle was stuck in the wiry part of his uneven beard. "You going crazy again?"

"Crazy? Again?"

"Don't act like you don't know what I'm talking about. Am I going to have to shove you in a VA hospital like your ex did?"

"What's making you say this?"

"You've been sitting there for three hours. Weren't you going to work?"

I looked at the Big Ben alarm clock, ticking loudly on my nightstand. It was only six p.m. "I don't have to be there for hours."

"Good. Then you can save some money and eat dinner here."

"Let's go to the Polish buffet instead."

"Bah. It's a waste of money."

"It's nine-ninety-nine for all you can eat."

"They raised the price."

"To what?"

"Ten-ninety-nine. It's a ripoff now."

"Let's go anyway. You can ride on the back of the motorcycle."

"Fuerte. Hecho in Peru." He thought about it for a moment. "Nah. I'd look like a girl riding on the back."

"We could catch a cab. An Uber."

"You made of money now?"

"No. I've hit the wall on waffles."

He thought about that for a moment. "Yeah. Me, too. Hang on a minute." He went into the kitchen and dialed up one of his neighborhood buddies who lived a few doors down, Eddy McGinty, my old crush's father. I could hear him soft-soaping him. "Let's catch up," he said. "My idiot son is in town for some reason," he said. "Yeah, the one from the Army. What other one do I got?" He listened for a moment. "Okay, you mind driving? Great! See you in a few."

I listened to him clomping back to my room. He peered in at me. "We got a ride. With McGinty. You remember him. You used to rub one out for his daughter every night."

"Thanks for the reminder. Yeah. I remember him."

I think, under all that hair, my father was smiling wolfishly. "She's still a hot little number. She's divorced. Bad news is, she's got a bratty little shit of a kid who needs a punch in the face."

"I don't want to hear about it."

"Ah, don't get excited."

There was a deafening tone and my father blipped out of existence for a moment. Only a tiny light the size of a firefly was left behind where his midsection would have been. An echoey and muffled voice in a nearby room said, "This is a test. For the next ten seconds, this is a test. If this had not been a test, there would have been no test. The test is ended. Thank you for your patience." My father appeared again, but now he was clean shaven and his hair was combed. His face was gaunt, sunken-in and gray. His cheekbones stuck out and his chin jutted. He'd been handsome once, like a nineteen-fifties cowboy actor, but now he'd been reduced to gristle and bone. "Where am I?" he asked me.

"Home," I said. "You were gone for a moment."

"Home," he said, trying it on. "Weren't we going to go out?"

"Yes," I said. "To the Polish buffet."

"Well, good. I'm hungry."

"Me, too. Do you mind if I use your phone?"

"It's not long distance, is it?"

"It's my ex. I need to let her know that my phone doesn't work and she should call your phone until I get mine fixed."

"All right. But don't take too long. I don't want to have to pay for long distance."

Did long distance even exist anymore? Hadn't the world been reduced to paying for minutes instead? I went into the kitchen. It was the same phone that had been in our house forever, a rotary dial phone made of harvest gold bakelite hanging on the wall. I picked up the receiver and dialed my ex-wife's number from memory. The phone made a horrible racket instead of ringing. Doo-doo-deet! "We're sorry, the number you have dialed is not in service at this time. Please check the number and dial again." I hung up and dialed it again and got the same result. I closed my eyes and saw the number in my memory. I was dialing the right number. I was sure of it. I dialed it again and got the same result. Something was going on. Something wrong. She couldn't change her number. I panicked a bit. I called directory assistance and asked for the number for Claire Derleth in Highland Park, Illinois. The operator said that there was no Claire Derleth in Highland Park, Illinois. "That can't be right," I said.

"Calm down, sir, or I will have to hang up."

"But she lives there. In Highland Park. My ex-wife."

"Maybe she changed her number. Maybe she doesn't want to hear from you. You ever think of that?" The operator's voice had changed. She sounded less like a professional person and more like someone who was sick of her ex-husband. "You should calm down. Go get a Coke out of the fridge. Drink it. Think about what you're doing with your life. Think about that. What should you be doing?"

"I know I screwed up. I told her I was sorry. I know that's not enough. I know that sometimes people have to let go. But I don't want to let go. I want things to be normal again. This has got me thinking about things that I'd rather not think about. And there's my daughter to think about."

"What's your daughter's name?"

"Annie."

"Don't you think that Annie would want you to be happy?"

"Yes."

"Try taking care of yourself for a while. Try becoming a better person. I can hear in your voice that you're not a bad guy. But you're no good to anyone if you can't be good to yourself."

"Everyone deserves a normal home. Even broken people."

"That's true. But sometimes normal isn't enough. You think about that for a while. I want you to close your eyes. Are your eyes closed?"

"Yes." I closed my eyes tight. I saw stars.

"Visualize yourself at your best. The best version of you. What's that person doing?"

I saw myself in front of an drafting table in a conex box in Iraq. I was drawing a graphic novel. Someone was beside me, providing the story. I couldn't see who it was. A fellow soldier? I knew that the two of us had moved into the conex box without anyone's permission. We'd stolen art supplies. Electricity. Lights. A fan. Was this a real memory? "I don't know," I said. My hands both shook, as they did when I thought about doing anything artistic. "I have to go."

"Thank you for calling Midwestern Bell," she said. She hung up and a piercing dial tone whirred out of the phone. I jerked the receiver away from my ear, recoiling from the noise. I hung up.

"How'd that go?" my father asked. He was standing beside me.

"Not well."

"Sort of like the rest of your life." A horn honked out front. "That's McGinty. Let's go."

My father put on a show for whatever Social Security agent might be hiding in the bushes. He clunked slowly out to Eddy McGinty's Ford Fusion, which looked like it might belong to a government agency. As we got closer to it, I realized that it was probably bought at an auction. The tires had no white walls. The wheels were unadorned by hubcaps. The car was painted an institutional gloss black. In raised letters on the side, I could see where "City of Cuyahoga Falls Public Works Department" had been painted over. The gloss black on the driver's door did not match the gloss black on the rest of the vehicle. I got in the back seat. My father sat shotgun after shoving his walker on the seat next to me.

"Where's the missus?" my father asked Eddy.

"She hates you. So, she's at home."

"I see," my father said. He thought of himself as a likable guy, but enough people had looked him in the eye and told him, "I hate you," that he'd long ago accepted that he was an acquired taste. Like exotic candy from the far east, maybe.

"How you doing?" Eddy McGinty asked me via the rearview mirror.

"I'm good," I lied.

47

"He's a veteran. Like us. Remember when we put down the insurrection?"

"You mean the ten cent beer riot? Yeah. That was a hoot."

They'd both served in the same Ohio Air National Guard unit. Eddy McGinty, I seemed to recall, was a gyroscopic service technician. That ended up translating into a civilian job at Hopkins Airport. "Working the system," my father called it.

I looked out the window, watched the neighborhood go by.

"Joe Ziska said he saw you today," Eddy said.

"Joe's full of shit," my father said.

"Not you, Larry. Phil."

My father turned around in his seat. "When did you have time to go get a beer?"

"When I took the motorcycle for a test ride."

"That old Fuerte? You still have that thing?" Eddy asked.

"Yeah. What of it?" my father said.

"Wasn't there a general recall? Like they spontaneously blew up or something?"

"I believe the recall said, 'May experience sudden explosive instances,'" my father said.

"And you're letting your son ride around on it."

"He's an adult. He can make his own choices."

"Wait a minute. I didn't know about the sudden explosions."

"Sudden explosive instances," my father said.

"Is that why you didn't want to ride on the back?"

"It's fine," my father said. "There's nothing wrong with that motorcycle. I've ridden on it plenty of times."

"Like when?" I asked.

"Plenty of times," he said. "Hey, ducks! Stop the car."

"I'm not stopping the car for ducks, Larry."

"Fine. Did I tell you that I got Phil into the guild? It's all secret and hush-hush, but he's in. He's been through the ritual."

"Some old fart hit me with a broom handle."

"Shut the fuck up!" my father shouted. "That's secret."

"It hurt like hell."

"I'm hungry," Eddy said. "Man, I'm gonna kill that buffet. Murder it."

"I hope they have sweet cheese pierogis tonight," I said.

"I'm gonna drain that bucket of Salisbury steak," Eddy said.

We pulled up and had to circle the parking lot three times to find a space. The place was packed. Outside hadn't changed a bit since I was a kid. The red brick and glass windows. The heavy ornate wooden door. I opened the door and the great scents washed over me. The same old sign hung swinging from the popcorn ceiling: PAY FIRST HERE, THEN EAT. My eyes watered. My mouth watered. Sauerkraut and cabbage rolls. Salisbury steak. Kielbasa. Pierogis swimming in butter. I used the credit card in my wallet to pay for all three of us. Stella, the old lady who'd run the place since the beginning of time, walked us to a booth in the back. She also ran an ice cream concession on Edgewater Beach during the summer. As we walked, I heard people shouting at my father, "Hey, Larry! What're you doing out?" "You owe me ten bucks!" "Mow your lawn!" "You cheat at pinocle!" "When did you finally shave?"

We temporarily sat down at the booth to await our waitress, who would take our drink order (ONE REFILL ONLY) and would clear each wave of plates after we filled and emptied them.

"Hey, Pop," said the waitress to the man sitting across from me, Eddy McGinty. I looked up and saw Patty McGinty, with her blond hair and pale skin, her blue-green eyes like the sea. She was dressed all in black like a thief.

I felt guilty and looked out the window. I saw a tramp next to Eddy's car, peering in through the windshield. Something had caught his eye. I knocked on the glass and shouted, "Hey, I see you!" I turned to Eddy. "Look at that bum. Looking at your car."

"It's fine," Eddy said. "I locked it up." He aimed his key fob at the car and pushed a button. The car made a horrendous racket and all its lights blinked, including the interior lights.

The tramp looked in at us, sitting all warm and cosy in the restaurant, and sighed. He stepped back from the car. I felt slightly guilty. Then I looked up at Patty and felt tremendously guilty and looked away.

"Is that Phil Derleth? Oh shit! You gotta be kidding me!" Patty said in her adorable lisp. "Don't you recognize me? We went to school together!"

"Hi, Patty," I said.

"Hi yourself. Get up here and give me a big old hug!"

"Um," I went, not moving.

"C'mon, you! Give me a hug!"

The whole restaurant grew silent. "Get up and give her a hug!" someone shouted. Then they were all shouting it. They chanted, "Hug! Hug! Hug! Hug!"

I had no choice in the matter. My father slowly got up and stepped out of the way. I slid over, stood up and then gave her the most awkward hug in the history of humankind, putting my arms around her but not really touching her and standing as far from her as I could while still creating the illusion of a hug, as the restaurant cheered. "This guy's a war hero!" Patty shouted over the cheers.

That's when I sat back down and slid back over as far as I could. If I could have evaporated into the wall, I would have. I looked out the window and the tramp was standing on the other side, his nose pressed against it, inches away from my face. He pointed at me and mouthed out, "You." He winked in a sinister manner, stood up straight, turned on his heel and walked away.

If anything, Patty was more beautiful at thirty. I tried not to see that. I tried to turn her into an outline of a person and not really look at her as she stood there and my ears and cheeks burned and my normal tinnitus turned into a deafening roar like a big summer storm rolling in off the lake.

My father elbowed me and the roaring stopped.

I blinked at him. "What?"

"She asked you what you want to drink, dummy."

I coughed and looked around. "A Coke."

"Was that so hard? Now let's go get some grub."

We loaded up, but I found myself picking at the food that I'd wanted so badly. The tramp and Patty had thrown me off my eating game entirely.

From the speaker in the ceiling, I heard Chaka Khan sing:

Love me right
What's the matter with you
Hold me tight
Why must I tell you what to do

Patty deposited the Coke in front it me and then placed a straw in a paper wrapper next to it. She smiled at me noncommittally, the way a waitress would smile at any paying customer. I thought about smiling back, but instead peered out the window looking for the tramp. He'd departed. The mercury vapor lamp on a post hovering above the parking lot glowed, drowning out the stars that had begun to peek out through the darkening sky. I realized Eddy was talking to me.

"Pardon me?" I went.

"I said, 'I'm sorry your mother couldn't be here tonight. She loved this place.'"

"Yes, she did," I said.

"He didn't come home for her. When she was dying."

I poked at the pierogi on my plate. I took a bite of sauerkraut. "I didn't. I was… I was working. I had to work."

"Had to work, he says. Big man."

"What do you do now that you're out of the Army?" Eddy asked.

"He got fired."

"I was a commodities trader. Pork bellies, mostly. It involves a lot of shouting."

"Some Army buddy of his hooked him up with the job."

"Crabby," I said. "He owed me. Anyway, that's what he thought."

"Why would he think that?" Eddy asked.

My father hadn't heard this story before. He'd never asked.

"I don't remember it, but we volunteered for convoy duty outside the wire. Actually, it was our medic who volunteered us. I was with Crabby on the back of a deuce-and-half, manning a fifty-cal. Someone fired a rocket at him, at us. I don't know. I…" I looked around, embarrassed. "Nothing."

"Not nothing," Eddy said. He'd stopped eating and put his fork down. He stared directly into me. "What happened?"

"I stepped in front of Crabby. The rocket hit me. It was a dud, I guess. Anyway, that's the story that Crabby told everyone. I don't remember it." I laughed. "Maybe I'm dead." I laughed some more. My own laughter sounded distant to me. Foreign.

"Maybe this is all the dream of a dead man. Wouldn't that be funny?"

"Calm down, son."

"Am I a man now?" I asked him. "Did I make it?"

"Calm the fuck down. People are staring." My father wouldn't look at me. He looked down at his plate. No one was staring. No one at all was paying any attention except the two old Ohio Air National Guardsmen. "Jesus H. Christ," my father mumbled. "Be quiet, dummy. Eat your food."

Eddy turned away, embarrassed. They look at me differently when they hear this story. They look at me all funny. That's why I don't tell it.

"I married Crabby's sister, too," I said nervously, my hands shaking. "And had a kid with her. Claire is beautiful. Our daughter is beautiful. We lived a normal life. Everything was normal in Illinois. Good and boring. Nothing wrong with boring. And there was a sweet little niece for Crabby to dote on. I guess that paid me off in full." I tried to look out the window, but all I saw now was my own reflection. My face was foreign to me. There was something off about it. Something missing. "That tramp. Where did he go?"

"They come and go," Eddy said.

"You're wasting money. Eat," my father said. He lowered his head to a couple of inches off his plate and shoveled the food in. Shoveled and shoveled.

HABITUAL FRIENDS

Riding the Fuerte was a noisy adventure, especially navigating around the foot-deep and foot-wide potholes that had proliferated between Kamm's Corners and North Olmsted. The headlight on the motorcycle grew stronger at higher speeds and dimmed when I pulled up to stoplights. Black smoke poured out of the tailpipe and rose into the dark and was carried ahead of me by tailwinds, creating vaporous shadows under swaying streetlights.

I knew the way to the Heartland Mall. I had it memorized from when I was a teenager.

I hung out there with my school buddies Milt Molina and Sam O'Hare. I call them buddies because we were friends of convenience. The three of us were scrawny knock-kneed virgins, unathletic pimple poppers with no girlfriends and no prospects of girlfriends. We were united in our long-distance adoration of Patty McGinty, with her blond hair and pale skin, her blue-green eyes like the sea. We did not speak openly about our adoration. We only occasionally whispered her name out loud, sometimes involuntarily. "Patty McGinty," one of us might say, at random, and the other two would gasp a bit and all three of us would sweat nervously until the spell was broken.

We hung out in Dragon's Dungeon, a D&D shop in the Heartland Mall, on those occasions when the three of us had time off from work. This happened about once a week on average. We'd buy supplies and then head over to one of our houses to play.

I worked for my father, hauling bricks and stones and mixing mortar. Sam worked at the Orange Julius in the Heartland Mall. Milt worked at a driving range in Parma, adjacent to Shaker Heights, handing out rented clubs and buckets of whacked to death golf balls. His father owned the place. Both Sam and Milt had two sisters each, who had nothing but contempt for the three of us. They wore candy-colored skintight clothes and listened to boy bands on their iPods. They chewed gum constantly, snapping it in their mouths. They giggled scornfully when we were around, hanging out at Milt's or Sam's house. We couldn't hang out at my house. My mother wouldn't allow it. We tried twice. It seemed democratic to give my house a shot.

"What are you doing?" my mother asked the first time we were over. She stood in my doorway, her hair in curlers, wearing her ratty old housecoat. "Something weird?"

When we tried to explain D&D to her, she concluded that it was, indeed, weird and possibly against the Church, and she wouldn't have it in her house. "I mean… elves? That's weird," she said. "I'm going to ask Father Bob about it. Get some sort of ruling. He went to Notre Dame, you know, so he's up on all the latest Church teachings. The Notre Dame in Indiana, the real one, not the one in Elyria." She retreated for a few minutes back to the living room, to her stories, which she blasted at max volume out of our antiquated Quasar TV set.

The second time we tried meeting at my house, my father was home. He denounced one of the characters on her favorite story as "Danny the Faggot." As in: "Did Danny the Faggot finally come out of the closet? Look at that fairy! He's got orange makeup on his cheeks."

"That's not makeup!" my mother shouted. "It's our crappy TV set that you're too cheap to replace! And why can't we get an air conditioner? It's hot in here, Larry. I'm boiling to death."

"It's not hot in here. Try going outside and working your ass off building walls for the ingrates that populate this town. Jesus H. Christ, Marie. Get a grip."

"Don't blaspheme around me, Lawrence Derleth. I won't hear you take the Lord's name in vain."

"I'm going to the garage. I need to work on something. I expect to see dinner on the table at six sharp."

"You're gonna work on that six-pack of Black Label, is what you're gonna work on. And listening to the Indians. That Tom Hamilton is too loud!"

"That's it. I won't stand here and listen to you besmirch the name of the greatest broadcaster in sports." The door slammed.

My friends and I looked at each other and silently decided to never come to my house again. At that moment, my mother appeared in the door. "Keep in down in here!" she shouted. "I have a migraine." She stomped down to the master bedroom and slammed that door.

"Let's go," I said, and it was the last time we hung out at my house.

I arrived at the Heartland Mall at eight-thirty. I still had time to walk around the mall and maybe get my phone looked at. There didn't appear to be many cars in the lot. I parked near the Buy and Bye, the northernmost anchor of the mall. I walked through the double set of glass-plated doors and into Electronics City, with its dozens of TV sets, all showing a cable news station. A pale man with burning eyes was saying something about America and how beset it was by those who would destroy it, from without and within. He was joined by a lean woman with white blond hair. The camera panned back to show off her tanned and athletic legs. In the top corner of the screen, an animated American flag flapped. The lower third of the screen had a flashing red light in the corner and a scroll along the bottom repeated, "ALERT ... ALERT ... ALERT..."

"Welcome to Buy and Bye," a man in a green polo shirt said to me.

"Thank you," I said.

"Is there anything that I can help you find this evening?"

"Oh. Um. No. No. I mean. No." I hadn't rehearsed this interaction in my head. I got confused. "I'm supposed to report here at eleven."

"You're a new associate?" he asked. He seemed concerned.

"Yes," I said.

He grabbed me by the shoulders, looked me in the eyes and said quietly but firmly, "Run."

"What?"

"Run. Get out of here. Don't come back. Don't make the same—" He stopped and backed away from me.

"Are you being helped?" a woman asked from behind me. "Satisfactorily helped, I mean. Like in a satisfactory manner?"

I turned around and looked down at a short woman, maybe five feet tall, wearing a green polo shirt, khaki trousers and gleaming white sneakers. Her auburn hair was splayed around shoulders. Her name tag said, ASTRID SOGAARD, ASST GEN MGR. My brain classified her as an officer.

"Yes, ma'am. I was just explaining to…"

"Roderick," said the man who told me to run.

"Roderick," I said. "That I'm supposed to report here at eleven tonight. He was welcoming me to the team."

"I hope that's what he was doing," Astrid Sogaard said, peering around me and glaring suspiciously at Roderick. "I certainly hope for his sake that that is what he was doing. I hope so. Roderick, is that what you were doing?"

"Yes, that's—"

"Good! Now, why don't you take a walk around the mall until ten-forty-five or so and then come right back here for your new employee indoctrination. Oh, we have a special surprise for all our new associates tonight! It's very exciting. You will be excited. I bet Roderick wishes he could be here for it, but he's not new, are you Roderick? You are not new. Not at all. If wishes were fishes, right Roderick?"

"Yes, ma'am. I sure do—"

"I bet you do. I bet you do." She sighed, thinking of the specialness of the overnight to follow. "Now, scoot, you new employee, you. Go on. Find your joy in the mall. But be back at ten-forty-five. So special! Tonight! So special!" She walked away.

Roderick placed a hand on my shoulder. "I told you to run." He shook his head sadly. "You ain't gonna. I can see that. Cruel circumstances have brought you to this low place. Where'd you serve, brother?"

"Iraq," I said. "Mostly burned shit in Al-Basrah province."

"This is worse."

"Worse than burning shit?"

"Much worse. But you'll see. Wait til the shit show tonight. If that don't get you running out of here, I don't know what will."

I didn't know what to say to that. "See you around, I guess."

"That you will."

I walked through the rest of the Buy and Bye. It was mainly composed of boxes of product that were stacked up twelve and fourteen feet high, everything from paper towels to TV's to the Juicy Juicer AS SEEN ON TV. A small drone buzzed around near the ceiling and crashed into one of the spotlights mounted up there. Sparks cascaded from the struck light and shoppers looked heavenward. The drone burst into flames and slammed into the terrazzo floor four feet in front of me. The camera on the drone buzzed and appeared to zoom in on me. I crouched down beside the drone and looked into the lens. A tinny voice came out of a small speaker next to the camera. "Help… me," I heard. The red light on the drone died out. A tiny spark flashed in the center of the drone and a wisp of smoke rose from its carcass. A janitor bot as big as a riding mover beeped and called out jocularly in a beefy voice, "Comin' through! Hey! Hey! Comin' through!" I stood up and stepped out of its way and it scooped up and consumed the little drone with a hearty crunch, leaving behind a shiny floor in the process.

I quickly left the Buy and Bye after that and entered the mall proper.

The mall was two levels. I decided that I would walk both. I discovered that most of the old stores were gone, replaced either by nothing—I peered through glass windows and pulled-down gates at hastily vacated stores with empty clothes racks and empty shelves and 75 PERCENT OFF signs on the floor—or by downgraded versions of what had been there before. A national chain bookstore had become "Nothing But Bibles!" The Hot Topic became a shop called "Make Your Own T-Shirt." The Discount Drug Mart became an advertising area for a cancer treatment center for rich people. The Claire's became "Maria's Too Cute Jewelry," with plastic mockups of actual jewelry on sale for a dollar. The Sports Authority became a place that sold off-brand mockups of actual baseball and football merchandise for five and ten dollars. I saw a sweatshirt for the "Cleveland Brawns," a basketball jersey for the "Cabs," and a baseball jersey for the "Injuns" with "Chief Yippee" on the sleeve.

The Dragon's Dungeon, surprisingly, was still open. I went in and was shocked to see Milt Molina standing behind the counter, apparently supremely bored. He gazed up and saw me, and it didn't register at first. He stared at me for a moment, his mouth open, and finally said, "Phil? Is that you?"

"Yes."

"Holy shit."

"You can say that again."

"I heard that you were, um. Like, uh. Not alive?"

"No. That was my mother."

"But didn't something happen to you?" He pointed up at his forehead.

"Yes. But I'm here now. How's it going? You bought the place, huh?"

"Yeah. My father bought it as a tax dodge after I graduated from Kent State. Degree in accounting."

We stood there for a while and he told me the story of his life. He kept interrupting himself, saying, "Pretty boring." He managed to get married. He met his wife in college in a creative writing class. The two of them were bitched out by the professor for writing Anne McCaffrey-esque swords and sorcery-type fiction. The professor kept telling them, "Write what you know." "So we did! Fucking dickhead!"

It was nice to see a familiar face. I told him that I was starting at the Buy and Bye that evening. "Good luck with that," he said.

"Yeah." I told him about Roderick.

"That dude's probably right. But you do what you have to in life. Right?"

"I guess," I said.

We both went silent and kind of stared at each other, embarrassed by the silence. Other than our teenage geekery, we had nothing in common. We probably didn't even like each other. I could see a future where we hung out forever out of habit, not enjoying each other's company.

I pulled out my phone and waved it around. "I gotta go take care of this. It may be broken."

"The Phone Store is three doors down that way," he said, pointing, relieved that I was leaving.

"Got it."

"Stay in touch," he said. He smiled in that uniquely noncommittal American way. "I'm glad you're alive."

"Thanks. Me, too." I followed his directions and came to the second liveliest store in the mall, other than the Buy and Bye.

The Phone Store was still kicking, even at nine p.m. The store was well lit, shiny and sterile, like a Stanley Kubrick movie set. A half dozen employees stood ready to assist, arrayed around the store. Six tables held six different iterations of phones and tablets, which was all they sold. A giant video wall in the back had talking head people blabbing about how much the phones and tablets had changed their lives. They looked like they believed it, too. My phone was expensive. I'd needed it when I was a commodities trader. It was part of that whole life, along with suits and ties and shouting a lot. A man screamed at one of the workers: "This is why everyone hates the Phone Store!" He stomped out past me. The worker, a roundish blob with chin whiskers, smirked cooly watching the enraged customer leave.

I pulled out my phone and kind of waved it at the employee. I'd rehearsed this conversation in my head on the motorcycle on the way in. "My phone isn't working," I said, just as I'd imagined saying it.

He rolled his eyes. "Go talk to him." He pointed at a man poking at a tablet.

I walked over to the man poking at a tablet. He looked post-collegiate. His hair was hip. He wore hip glasses. All the employees wore hip t-shirts. A woman on the giant video wall said, "Organized. I was never organized. And then…" Hip droning music played over the top of her. The phone rotated where her face had been. It was ten feet tall and gleaming. "What?" the hip phone employee went.

"My phone isn't working," I said.

"What's wrong with it?"

"It won't turn on."

"Won't turn on."

"Yes."

"Did you back your phone up to the cloud?"

"I think so."

"You think so." He seethed with contempt. He wouldn't look up from the tablet. He kept poking at it. "Stand over there." He pointed with his poking hand.

I walked over to the middle table of the first three and stood. Five minutes turned into twenty. Another man, equally hip, walked over to me. "Yes?" he went. At least he was looking at me.

"My phone isn't working," I said.

"What's wrong with it?"

"It won't turn on."

"That happens." He took the phone from me. "Did you use an authorized charger last time you charged your phone?"

"Yes," I said. "I used the charger that came with the phone."

"So you didn't buy the upgraded charger. Because this is a 2015 model. It came with a 2015 model charger. But the operating system was upgraded to require a new charger. Do you understand?" He spoke to me in a tone that suggested that I was a particularly dim kindergartner.

"So how can I make the phone work again?"

He sighed. "This is a known issue. You should have received a message on the phone telling you to upgrade your charger. Did you buy Phone Care when you bought the phone? What's your number?"

I told him my number. He typed it into the tablet he'd brought with him. "You did buy Phone Care. We'll replace your phone right now. But you'll have to buy the upgraded charger."

"Okay."

He walked away without another word. One minute became twenty. He returned with a new phone and unboxed it. He popped the sim card out of the old phone and put in it the new one. He had me sign into the phone and it immediately started downloading all of my data. It chimed when it was done. He handed me the new charger. I handed him my credit card and hoped it would work one last time. It did after a long, lingering minute in which I prepared myself to be mortified. I gasped out my relief a little too audibly and the clerk smirked contemptuously and walked away. My new phone chimed. I opened up my email and the receipt was in there.

"I'm done?" I asked out loud.

No one answered.

EMBRACE THAT HAPPINESS

There were maybe a dozen of us standing there in the middle of the Buy and Bye, awaiting our orders, after all of us had gone through in-processing. Out of habit, we all stood at modified parade rest. We were each told to stand on a star, because we were already "star associates." We were all veterans. That much was clear. I showed up early and Roderick explained to me that most of the new employees these days were veterans. We didn't complain much, understood that life was a losing proposition, had health care through the VA, so didn't ask for that, and understood institutional life. The doors shut behind us and locked shut with an authoritative clang. A buzzer sounded. The lights dimmed and a spotlight shown on the floor in front of us. Music swelled. Timpani. Horns. An unsubtle string section. An electric guitar ripped off a single, whanging note.

"Are! You! Ready!" Astrid Sogaard's amplified voice asked. She was somewhere out of sight.

We all studied at each other. We were waiting for one of us to take charge and maybe shout out a "Woo!" or a "Yeah!"

"Woo!" Astrid Sogaard went from her hidden position. Her voiced echoed hollowly around the mostly empty store.

There was a loud pop and some confetti shot out of the floor. We all hit the deck, face down. In front of each of our faces was a key.

"Do you see the key next to your nose? Pick it up! Later on, one of you will be the lucky winner if your key fits the lock!" Astrid Sogaard's amplified voice told us.

I peered around at my fellow associates. All of us had managed to retain bladder control. So that was a positive. I picked up my key and slipped it in my pocket. We all managed to stand up again.

"And now! Give a warm Buy and Bye welcome! To! Zinn Prak Dopp! Woo!"

I remembered Zinn Prak Dopp. He was a guru who showed up on my mother's stories. The networks would work him into the plots. On the story that took place mostly in a hospital, he was a patient. On the story that took place in a town filled with snippy people, he was the coffee shop barista.

"Are they really going to teach us how to meditate?" said a nearby associate. "This is some bullshit."

The floors were obscenely clean thanks to the beefy-voiced janitor robot, so there was no need to dust ourselves off, though we all did. Old habits are hard to break.

A man of medium height and medium build walked into the shaft of blinding light in the center of the store. He was dressed in a slate t-shirt and slate trousers with slate tennis shoes laced with slate laces. His hair was buzzed off. He looked like no one. He looked like everyone. He was both masculine and feminine. He could have been thirty or fifty-five. "I see you!" he said, pointing in my general direction. I flinched. "I see you!" he said, pointing slightly away from me. "I see all of you. I see you equally. I see you evenly. I want to show you something." He pulled out a small change purse from his pocket. "See this? Every day, I put a coat of wax on it. And every day, I put a coat of wax on my BMW M4. And every day, I put a coat of wax of my kitchen counter. Why do I say this? I give everything the same attention as if I was giving Sweet Baby Jesus himself a bath. Nothing and no one should be treated more carefully than anything or anyone else. A bitching car, a kitchen counter and, this! A change purse! Hah-hah-hah! Are all the same! Can you see it, like I see…" He spun round and pointed at another associate. "You? Oh, hah-hah!" He put the coin purse away and walked over to a platform. He stood on it and it rose up half way to the distant ceiling. The spotlights never left him. "To be an effective associate means that you must master your perceptions. You must see everyone and everything as exactly equal. The turtle and the butterfly. The sky and the fiery pit. It is all the same. When you eat your lunch during your extended twenty-minute break period, experience the lunch. Luxuriate in the crunch of the toasted bread, the sweetness of the tomato, the savoriness of the hummus. It is all of a piece and yet each element brings its own elan to the symphony." He swept his hands out. "Like you. Let's do an exercise. I want you all to repeat after me… Whoa! Whoa! Whoa!"

"Whoa. Whoa. Whoa."

"Oh, my. Seriously? Oh, we all have much to learn tonight. Good thing I brought these delicious gummy fruit snacks. But I will only give a packet of delicious gummy fruit snacks to those who truly participate. So say it with me: Whoa! Whoa! Whoa!"

About half participated this time.

It went on and on. Eventually, he tossed fruit snacks at us randomly.

"Am I crazy? Are you crazy? Oh, but we all must be a little bit crazy, mustn't we? Truly, only the crazy, the thinkers out of the box, can stretch their imaginations to fulfill our customers' dreams. We must live each day as if it were our last, and also the last day of our customers' lives. Walk up to each of them and treat them as if they were your own mother, father, wife, daughter. Dying in front of you! Look into their eyes and dream their dreams with them. What's their last wish? Is it for a reasonably priced Juicy Juicer as seen on TV? We have to move them. Buy and Bye bought too many and now they must go. Sleep at night thinking of those dreams, your customers' dreams. Fly in your imagination. True happiness can't be found in hiding in the breakroom. It can only be found in the eyes and imaginations and dreams of the people who walk through our doors every day. Don't wish to be happy here at Buy and Bye. Once you merely wish that, the wish dies. Be happier at Buy and Bye. Be the happiness. Do you know that once you embrace that happiness, you can do anything? Who believes me? Who truly believes me?"

I was stunned to see every hand but mine shoot up. I raised my hand carefully, not wanting to draw interest from the guru. But I was too slow. The platform lowered down to our level. The guru walked over to me and suddenly embraced me. I didn't know what to do with that. No man had ever thrown his arms around me before. He whispered in my ear, "Oh, my brother. I am shocked at you. Shocked that you cannot love. Not even yourself. And you smell like sauerkraut. It's heavenly." He let me go and I staggered backward. "Everyone, right now, sit down on the floor. Yes, even you, my friend," he said, pointing at me. "Everyone, right now, close your eyes. Close them. Now imagine yourself as a feather. A feather dancing in a breeze as the sun rises over a gigantic swelling ocean and you are ever so slightly floating above a sandy beach. Oh, yes! Yes!"

I opened my eyes and everyone, including Zinn Prak Dopp, was floating a few feet above the sales floor, levitating in the air. I was not.

Zinn Prak Dopp smiled devilishly at me. "Tsk, tsk. It doesn't matter. You're a dreamer. Where's your dream partner, dreamer? Most dreamers have one." He placed his index finger up against his lips and made the slightest shush. "Okay now! Everyone imagine floating down, down, down onto the sugary sand until you make a tiny indentation, barely perceptible to the human eye." I watched everyone drift downward until they were seated on the ground again. "Very good. Open your eyes. You each get a packet of these most delicious fruit snacks. Clap for yourselves. A round of applause for my best students." He leapt to his feet and tossed the fruit snacks to everyone but me. He crouched down in front of me and handed me the packet, placing it directly into the palm of my hand while maintaining unblinking eye contact. He stood up. He said to the associates while slowly rotating round, levitating several inches above the floor, "Anyone who learns to live well, will learn to die well. Don't you think? Living well means living in the exact present moment, the right now. The right here. Don't hang onto your past. Your past is a creation of a fiend! The fiend is the fictional past self that you made up to please the most horrible master that is you. Plant the seeds of compassion within yourself. The first object of your compassion should be you, you, you. I look around and I see beauty. I see you and you and you. I see the terrazzo floors. I see the boxes and boxes of beautiful product. I see sunsets. I see butterflies and clouds. I see Juicy Juicers as seen on TV. They are all equally beautiful." He levitated higher and higher. "Suffering comes from wanting things to be different than they are. You must accept things as they are, as they are supposed to be. Joy can be found in the mundane. Where does our real future lie? In selling a plasma TV in Electronic City. In helping a customer discover the best refrigerator for her price range. Wanting more than what you can reasonably get corrodes the soul and only creates heartache and pain and it makes you into a killjoy that no one at work will want to share a sandwich with. Fly, be free of that want. Fly, be true to your true self, your present self. Soar with me! Soar! Let go of your mind and only then will you know your mind. The person who thinks they can win is the person who can win." He was nearly touching the ceiling by this time. He pulled a light bulb from seemingly nowhere, unscrewed the light bulb that the drone had destroyed and replaced it with the new one in his hand. He descended quickly and landed gently on the tips of his toes. He tossed me the blown-out bulb. The bulb dissolved into black ash in my hands. "That ends my lesson. You'll all be asked to fill out a survey concerning the lesson tonight. If you mark all fives for this lesson, your karma will swell. If you do not, you'll be asked to explain why not during a Buy and Bye 'bull' session. Thank you, and have a great rest of the night."

I clapped my hands and the ashy dust drifted off them and then I wiped my hands on my pants.

Astrid Sogaard walked among us handing us electronic tablets. Mine looked like it had seen better days. There was a chip missing out of one of the corners and a thin green line ran the length of the screen. The lights slowly came up until the store was filled with blinding white light. "You have five hours to complete the fifteen tasks that the tablet will give you. If you do not complete the tasks, you will have to complete them on your break time during your first week of work. On your mark. Ready, set, go!"

The words "Tap here," appeared on my tablet. I tapped.

The animated tasks ran from helping a mother find the restroom so she could change her baby's diaper and preventing her from using the opportunity to steal a phone, to figuring out the best way to stack boxes in a limited space on a sales floor. In each scenario, we were helped along by an anime version of Bert Bacon, the founder of Buy and Bye, who would end each lesson by recounting a similar problem that he'd had in nineteen-sixty-seven in Omaha, Nebraska at the original Buy and Bye Discount Super Store and Hefty Boy Feed Lot. Bert Bacon would start off each video by saying, "Hello honored veterans, and others, I'm Bert Bacon..." The anime Bert had huge, expressive eyes and wore bib overalls. When I did a good job on a lesson, he'd say,

"You deserve an ear of corn!" and he'd toss one into a bucket in the corner of the screen. I finished with about fifteen minutes to spare and earned five ears of corn in the process. It didn't hurt that I'd wandered the store while playing the games/lessons and found a dusty gaming chair to sit in for the duration.

Astrid Sogaard found me in my gaming chair and took the tablet without a word. I stood up and stretched. I saw the sun coming up through the chain mail screen that was on a timer and had come down over the glass doors leading to the outside world. I was ready to go home and go to bed. We each walked up to the door and Astrid Sogaard waved a metal detector wand over us and gave us each a light frisking, checking our socks, mostly. She checked the little St. Sebastian's backpack that I hadn't taken off all night. I'd learned about his process in the lesson titled, "Shrinkage: What is it and how do we prevent it?" An alarm bell sounded and the chain mail screen raised automatically back to the recess in the ceiling. My fellow associates filed out one-by-one. I was the last in line. "Wait," Astrid Sogaard said. "Stay here."

I felt my heart kick into gear, begin to race uncontrollably. This happened on occasion. Sometimes it happened for no reason at all. It was involuntary. My VA shrink in Chicago called it a panic disorder. He prescribed drugs to keep it under control. I had five or six different drugs in amber vials that I either took once or twice a day, or I took "as needed." I tried doing the visualization exercises that the VA therapist (different from the doctor) had taught me. I never found that visualization exercises worked for me. I suppose that not levitating had underlined that.

Astrid Sogaard reappeared with Zinn Prak Dopp. "Doppy needs a ride to the airport," Astrid Sogaard said.

Zinn Prak Dopp smiled at me. "I won't bite. I promise. No shop talk either."

"I don't have a car. I have a motorcycle," I said.

"Fine," Astrid Sogaard said. She reached into the pocket of her khakis and produced a key fob. "Just bring the Buy and Byte Computer Repair Plus Mobile back in one piece." She walked us to the door. "It's right over there."

It was the tiniest car I'd ever seen in real life. It was painted like an old fashioned ambulance, with red crosses on the side and a red bubble flasher on the top. My heart banged like a runaway machine gun. The two of us crammed ourselves into the cockpit of the thing. We were squished together inside, both of our heads scraping against the ceiling of the tiny car. I looked for an ignition switch. A button.

"Just step on the accelerator," Zinn Prak Dopp said. "She'll go. She's a goer. I ride in one of these once a week, right after a new employee orientation."

I did stomp on the accelerator and the little car zipped along. We were about ten miles from the airport, just enough time for an uncomfortable silence to fill the car as I drove along.

The signs for the airport came up none-too-quickly, but when they did, Zinn Prak Dopp decided to speak. "Can I tell you a secret?"

"Fuck."

"Does that mean 'yes.'"

"Just say whatever it is you have to say. What airline are you flying?"

"United. The friendly skies. Hah-hah. Anyway. What I was going to say was—"

A cab cut me off and kind of triggered me again. "Son of a bitch!" I shouted. "Motherfucker!"

"Anyway," Zinn Prak Dopp said. "About that key in your pocket..."

"What?" I said. Our upper arms were touching—my right, his left—that's how crammed into the car we were. He had no luggage. He had nothing but the stupid gray clothes on his back.

"You are a dreamer, not a lev—"

"I don't give a shit about levitating."

"I was about to say... um."

"Okay," I said.

"The thing is..."

"Out with it. We're nearly there." My heart felt like it might explode. It wouldn't stop racing and pounding, like an angry man kicking in the door of his wife's lover, the man who'd stolen her away from him, the man who broke up his normal family and normal life and sent him into a downward spiral that led him to the VA nut hutch and eventually back to his father's house, back to Ohio, to work in a fucking Buy and Bye and not levitate for some shitty guru for fuck's sake. I pulled up to the curb. "We're here."

He opened the door and stumbled out of the car, losing his balance for a moment and then righting himself. "What I wanted to say was—"

"I could give a rat's ass." I stomped on the accelerator and zipped away from the curb, leaving him standing there. "This is. This. Is. This is bullshit!" I shouted as I pounded on the steering wheel and sped away from the airport, back to the Buy and Bye to return their miniature car. I coughed and coughed like I always did when my heart raced. I thumped my chest with a closed fist trying to make it stop. I pulled over and dry-heaved. There was nothing in my stomach but a tincture of thin green goop. "Fuck!" I shouted, pacing on the side of the road. I nearly threw the key fob away. I got back in the car and drove it to the Buy and Bye. I walked in the front door and Roderick was there.

"You look like shit," he said.

"Here," I said. I tried to hand him the key fob.

"No. Uh-uh. Not me. Don't even try to hand me that thing."

"Who then?"

"Day manager. He's in the office."

"No fucking way," I said. I dropped the key fob on the ground in front of him. "I can't deal with this shit for a second longer." I turned and walked out the door, out into all that sunshine. Fucking sunshine.

C'mon heart. Stop this shit. Stop it. Stop. Stop. Stop.

A GOOD SIGN

I rolled the Fuerte over to an area congested with dumpsters. These were temporary cardboard dumpsters, so they didn't have as much of that specific dumpster odor as the usual dumpsters. Not as many flies, either. I was waiting for my episode to pass.

I reached into my pocket, absently searching for an amber pill bottle that no longer existed, sitting there on the Fuerte, and found the key that I'd picked up off the floor at the beginning of the night. What happened to the contest? Wasn't there supposed to be a mystery box with a prize in it? Did I miss the drawing to see who would open the box? Was there ever a box to begin with?

I heard the snapping before I saw them. It was rhythmic, almost soothing. Snap! Snap! Snap! Snap! And then the tramps emerged from behind the dumpsters, snapping their fingers in unison. They were filthy beyond any kind of recognition, save for one of them. He was the tramp from the Polish buffet the evening before. The tramps crouched low, like Groucho Marx, in a walking squat. They stepped along with their snapping. All of them staring at me. They stopped and the snapping stopped. They stood in a circle around me, north-south-east-west. The one directly in front of me, the cleanest one, said, "I marked this one last night. I know a good oh-neg when I see one, oh my brothers."

"I see that," the one directly behind me said.

"You're mad, just like us. But it's not really madness, is it? You can see what everyone else ignores," the cleanest tramp said.

"He's filled with blood. A big blood bucket, ripe for the picking," the one to my left said.

"Good thing I'm a licensed phlebotomist," the one to my right said. He reached into his mud-crusted trench coat and produced a long needle, the kind used on mastiffs who need rabies shots.

"Fifty bucks a pint for oh-neg," the cleanest tramp said. "That's the going price."

"We should rush him before he gets an idea in his head," the one behind me said.

"This one? This one has no ideas in his head. You can tell when you squint into his eyes," the cleanest tramp said.

My heart decided, in this moment, that I would be calm. It slowed way down. Time slowed way down, too. Time dilation can be a friend to the man in trouble. Like when that rocket came my way in Iraq. I was remembering snatches of it now, in that parking lot. I had what seemed like minutes to push Crabby to the ground and stand in front of the rocket. There was someone else, too! I'd saved two lives. I had so much time that I had time to think about what I was doing. Pop, no kick. A thump in the chest. A flower of an explosion blooming. The sun and sky. Doc leaning over me. Every fractured microsecond was embroidered into my memory, taking up the same space as entire years. But, that said, huge chunks of those microseconds were missing. There was something or someone... The second someone. I shook my head. "Get some," I said aloud, unstraddling the motorcycle, standing next to it. I have no fighting stance, so I stood there, my fists barely clenched, not braced for impact, but ready to fight just the same.

"Top of the food chain, we've conquered nature, and yet some of us still starve," said the cleanest tramp. "We just want our rightful place at the table, metaphorical or otherwise. We'll take it by force if necessary."

"I am for constitutional monarchy," said the tramp to my right. He played with his giant needle.

"As am I," said the tramp to my left. "I want a king to burn."

"To set alight," the cleanest man said. "On a spit."

"Burn the king. Burn him and all his children," the tramp to my rear said. "Burn the parliament down. And all the parliamentarians."

"Yes," the tramp to my right said. "That's what I want. All of that."

"And his blood," the cleanest tramp said. "Right now, I want his golden blood. I want fifty bucks."

But before they could rush me, a stray dog came trotting out from behind one of the temporary dumpsters. She lunged at the lead tramp, gripped his left ankle with her jaws and flipped him onto his back. Her mouth was filled with blood. She was a graceful dog, black and white furred, and built muscularly, solidly, her ears standing straight up on her head. She charged at the tramp to my right, who sprinted away. The other two ran off. The cleanest tramp managed to get to his feet.

"Don't say, 'This isn't over,'" I warned him.

"I won't," he said, hopping mostly on one foot. "It is. It's over. I only do easy pickings. Didn't know about your stray." He stumbled away.

The stray trotted up to me and stuck her head under my hand. I petted her. She had one brown eye and one blue eye. Her mouth was wet with the tramp's blood. I crouched down and petted her some more. She made a sound like "Moof."

"Thank you, thank you," I told her. "You're a good dog. The best." I've always gotten along better with dogs than I have people. I was equally heartbroken when Omar died as when my own mother died. That sounds horrible, but it's true.

The dog wore a braided collar around her neck. A tag attested that her shots were up-to-date. Another simply had her name on it, "Katie."

"Hello, Katie," I said. "Can I take you home? Where do you live?" I blinked and the dog was replaced by a woman. It was like watching one PowerPoint slide transition to another one, but without the fancy wipe. Click. She was on one knee, her nose nearly touching mine. We stood up together.

"It's you," she said, her voice shaking. "It's really you."

"Um, sure."

"Wait. Wait. No. You don't see me, do you?" She tilted her head to the side.

"I see you. Do you want that ride?"

"Thanks," she said. "I'd like a ride." She spat the tramp's blood onto the black parking lot surface. She smiled at me hopefully. "So you really don't remember me? Because you're looking at me just like you did the last time I saw you, which wasn't good." She reached over and lightly touched my forehead with her index finger and then withdrew her hand.

"What?" I went, taking a step back. I looked into her eyes and one was brown and the other blue. "Do I know you, Katie? I don't think so." I shook my head no.

"That's my name. At least you got that part." She played with the choker around her neck with the two tags on it. She had on a one-piece outfit that was like a combination of shorts and a t-shirt with a built-in belt around her waist. It was brown and white, and stained. There was an iron-on decal of Luba and Maggie from *Love and Rockets* on the t-shirt part of her outfit. They were dressed up as Batman and Robin. On her feet were a pair of faded-red low-top basketball shoes with dirty white laces. Her hair was jet black and shiny, and hung down nearly to her shoulders. She was slight and muscular. She had a street kid vibe to her, but she was my age. I knew some former street kids when I was in the Army. She reminded me of them. "Come on. Let's get on your motorcycle. Vroom, vroom. Let's go." She clapped her hands. Her fingernails were clipped short, but dirty. I handed her my helmet and she put it on. "It fits. That's a good sign. I like good signs." I flipped down the rear pegs.

"I'm Phil."

"I know who you are. But I guess you don't remember me. You will."

"What do you mean?"

"You'll figure it out. We'll figure it out together. Take me home. To your home."

I got on the bike and kicked it over. Black smoke rose into the air. "Sorry about that."

"Don't apologize. Not to me, anyway. I don't like apologies." She sat on the bike behind me and wrapped her arms around my midsection. "Let's go."

I revved the engine and zipped the motorcycle out from behind the cardboard dumpsters and into the parking lot proper. It was mostly empty. It was early. Very early. I got out onto the road and gunned the engine. It blatted out an industrial amount of black smoke as I navigated the potholes again.

Somewhere after we crossed into Kamm's Corners, we saw the accident. The rear of an old Chevy Impala, a mid-nineteen-seventies model by the look of it, was jutting up out of a massive pothole. The rear tires spun gently and blue-gray vapor poured out of the exhaust pipe in the rear. I saw myself and Katie reflected in the rear bumper as I pulled up to it. Katie hopped off the motorcycle, took off the helmet and handed it to me. She jumped into the pothole. She pulled on the door handle.

A moment later, Officers Smith and Jones appeared behind us, the lights on their police cruiser flashing.

Smith clapped a beefy hand on my back, startling me. "Something about you and crashed cars, isn't there?"

"Will this one burn?" Jones asked. "Stay tuned to find out."

Katie had already jumped into the massive pothole to try to rescue the people inside the car. "There's no one in here!" she called up.

"Who's that?" Smith asked.

"A stray," Jones said. "By the look of her."

Katie leapt out of the hole. She dusted off her knees. "Oh," she said, spooked by the two law officers. "Police." She backed up.

"Don't be afraid," Jones said. She took a knee and made a little clacking sound with her tongue. "Come here, girl. I won't hurt you. There's a good girl. C'mere."

Katie whined a moment, and for a moment she was a dog again, but only for a second or two. She stood up. "No," she said. "You won't get me." She became a dog again and ran off, sprinting into traffic and nearly getting hit by a rusty Chevy Cavalier, which slammed on its brakes. The driver honked and swore.

"You shouldn't pick up strays," Smith said. "They bite."

"I've seen that one around. She'll turn up again," Jones said. "And when she does, animal control will get her."

"We've got a tow truck on its way," Smith said. "Nothing to see here. Move along."

I got back on my motorcycle, put the helmet on and kicked the bike over. In the tiny, oval rearview, I watched Smith and Jones wave their hands in front of their faces as black smoke filled the air. I pulled away before they thought about ticketing me again. Two streets over, I saw Katie, now human again, standing on the side of the road. I pulled up next to her and she got on behind me. She wrapped her arms around me and I quickly got her back to my father's house.

After I pulled the Fuerte into the driveway, she got off the motorcycle and ran over to the back yard. She opened the gate and went inside. She sprinted in a wide arc around the backyard, stopped, dropped to her knees and sniffed the ground next to the birdbath. She got up, dusted her knees off, and walked over to the fence, where I was standing, watching her.

"Omar," she said. "That's where Omar is."

"Yes," I said.

"You told me about him. A long time ago."

"A car hit him."

"After your uncle let him out. He liked you." She tilted her head. "Do you mind if I stay here for a little while? I like your yard. It's not too roomy, but roomy enough. It smells nice."

"I don't mind."

"Can you get me some water? Maybe something to eat?"

"Yes. You can come inside if you like."

"I don't like the indoors these days. I feel cramped in there. Trapped."

"Okay," I said. "I'll go get you something."

She walked over to the birdbath and sniffed at the bubbling, dark water. "This smells fun. Interesting."

"Don't drink that. It's not healthy."

"Okay." Would she remember not to when she was a dog?

I went inside. My father was making a batch of what could only be described as Christmas waffles. They were red and green. He was putting crisscrosses of icing on top of them. "They were supposed to be orange and brown. I'm not sure what happened," he explained. "Who was on the back of your motorcycle? Girl from work?"

"Yeah." I thought about it. "Sort of." I thought some more. "No."

"Which is it?"

"She saved me from some tramps who dabble in selling blood," I said. "She bit one of them."

"Tough girl," my father said. He handed me an extra plate with an extra waffle on it. "For her. Invite her in."

"She doesn't want to come inside."

"Shy?"

"Something like that."

"I read about those tramps in the *Plain Dealer*. Big network of them trafficking in stolen blood. You're lucky."

"I guess," I said. I didn't feel lucky most of the time. I filled up a bowl with water.

"Who's that for?" my father asked.

"Katie."

"Who's Katie?"

"The one who saved me from the tramps."

"Right. She's not a stray, is she? There've been a lot of them around lately. We got a flyer from the police the other day. You forget that?"

"No. I haven't forgotten. And no, she's not a stray."

"You sure about that? There's some little shit who calls himself 'El Chicharrón.' He's the leader. They're all feral as hell. Undisciplined. They bite. They hang out in front of the tavern. They cadge drinks. Joe has to chase them off with a bucket of water."

"She's not a stray." I pushed through the door and walked around the house to the back yard. My father followed behind me.

"She's a stray," he said. Katie was a dog again, scratching her ear with her back paw and making a guttural noise. "Jesus H. Christ. You've got no sense. Picking up strays."

"Can she stay?"

"This house is yours as much as it is mine. Your call." He walked back toward the house, remembered himself, and limped the rest of the way.

I opened the gate and set the plate with the waffle down along with the dish of water. Katie sniffed skeptically at the waffle and then lapped up some water. She eventually ate the waffle, wolfing it down in three bites. I sat down on the ground next to her and petted her for a while. In the VA hospital, a Mister Rogers-like man used to bring a shaggy dog into my ward. I would always monopolize the time with the dog. I'm not sure anyone else was all that interested anyway. I whispered all sorts of secrets to that dog. Dogs are better than we are. Most of them are kind. They love without condition.

I whispered to Katie, "Thank you, thank you, thank you." I told her she was a good girl. She rolled over and I rubbed her belly, which was gnarled and matted. I went into the garage and found Omar's old grooming kit, stored in a shoebox on a shelf. I came back out and combed all of the mats out of her fur. I combed out her tail. She was patient with me. I was apologetic when I pulled some of the mats apart with the comb and brush. She yipped once or twice. When I was done, I took all the fur that I'd combed out of her and put it in the trashcan inside the garage. I put away the grooming kit. I tossed around a florescent green tennis ball in the backyard for her. There wasn't a whole lot of room, but enough for her to get some exercise. She finished up the water, so I went inside with the dry bowl to get some more water.

"You still horsing around with the stray?" my father asked, his voice distant and echoey. He was sitting on the couch with the paper in his lap, not looking at me. His body had a light sheen of static all around it, like he wasn't quite coming in. If he'd had an antenna atop his head, I would have attempted to adjust it.

"She needs me," I said.

"She'll break your fucking heart. Isn't your heart broken enough?"

"At least she didn't have any ticks on her. I didn't see any fleas either."

"You're gonna regret this. You should get some shuteye. When are you supposed to go back to work?"

I checked my phone. "They haven't texted me my schedule yet."

"I'm gonna go over and check out that job today."

"It's gonna take forever to get there the way you walk."

"I'm getting rid of the walker. I want to get back to work."

"You sure about that?"

"Yeah, I'm sure. You keep on going in to that place. Buy and Bye. Whatever. I'll go do what I do."

"You know your back is actually fucked up, don't you? Even if you can walk, you probably shouldn't do heavy labor any more."

"Shut up and mind your own business, dummy. And I'll mind mine." He faded away completely for a moment and then came back. "Go give your dog more water."

"You need to go to a doctor or something, dad. You're not coming in anymore. You're fading."

"You think I don't know that?" he snapped, shifting on the sofa to look over his shoulder at me. I could see right through him. The TV clicked on. It let out a mournful whine while it warmed up. After it did so, I saw a barbershop quartet on it, singing in perfect harmony, "You'd look better with rice pudding...rice pudding in your hair. Bum, bum, bum. Rice pudding in your hair. Bum, bum, bum. Rice pudding in your hair. Bum, bum, bum." It spooked me, so I left the room.

I took the filled bowl back into the yard, but Katie was gone. The gate was open. Did I leave it open? "Katie!" I called out. "Katie!" I thought about the police nabbing her. Animal control. Then what? Would they put her down? The thought panicked me.

I set down the bowl and walked around the neighborhood calling out her name. I jogged from street to street. "Katie! Katie!"

There was something about her. Something important.

NEEDS WORK

After jogging approximately four miles in circles around the neighborhood, I came home to an empty house, showered, and crawled into bed. The wind howled outside, waking me. I looked out my bedroom window at the backyard, and it was dusted over with a late season snow. I closed my eyes again and awoke in the late afternoon. My feet were warm, and I realized it was because Katie was curled up at the foot of my bed. She was wearing a pink collar that had the same two tags on it. Her fur was much cleaner. She smelled like snow. She opened her eyes and looked overjoyed to see me. She licked my face. "How'd you get in here?" I asked her.

She was human again in a blink, dressed in a mostly clean pink dress with worn-down sneakers on her feet. She kissed me on one cheek and caressed my other cheek with a free hand. "I missed you."

"I went looking for you, but you left."

"I got spooked. I heard your dad arguing with you. I remembered what you told me about him."

"My father."

"Omar didn't like him. Remember?"

"I remember. But how—? How'd you get in?"

"Your mother let me in."

I think my jaw dropped a bit. "My… mother?"

"She's in the kitchen." Katie slid off the bed and took me by the hand. I realized I wasn't wearing any clothes.

"I need to get dressed."

Katie said, "Okay," and she sat down on the rug in the middle of my bedroom.

"I'm naked."

"I don't mind," she said. "I always wondered what you looked like naked." She blushed. She smiled shyly.

I hesitated for a moment and then gave up. I got up out of bed and went back into my closet, dug through the box, and put on more high school clothes— a pair of worn out tightie-whities, ripped jeans, a Promise Ring concert t-shirt, and mismatched socks. Katie stood up and impatiently paced while I laced my sneakers on my feet. Everything fit better than it had a decade before, even though I'd matured considerably since my teenage years.

"Are you done yet? Can we go?" she asked. She didn't wait for my answer. She grabbed my hand and pulled me behind her.

My mother was in the kitchen, obsessively cleaning up. She was scrubbing down the waffle iron with steel wool. "Your father let this place go," she said. She wouldn't turn around. She wouldn't look at me.

I walked over and tried to touch her, but my hand disappeared as it grew closer to her. "Mom. Mom, I can't touch you."

"Your father can't be bothered to clean anything." She said, "your father," like he was my fault.

"Mom, what are you doing here?"

"It's rude to point out someone's mortality status," she said. "You didn't hear me calling you dead when you came back, did you?"

"I'm not dead," I said.

"Sure," she muttered. "You're not dead. Neither am I."

"Mom. Mom! Will you look at me? Why won't you look at me?"

"I'll look at you. But you have to go over to where your dog is standing."

I turned and looked. Katie was still human. She made a little sound in the back of her throat. "Ooof. Ooof." I backed up without taking my eyes off my mother. I stood next to Katie. She put her arm around my waist and leaned into me a bit. She trembled a bit. I didn't flinch away from her like I do almost everyone else who tries to touch me. She felt familiar.

Mom turned around. She had the waffle iron, covered in suds, in her hands. "Do you even know how angry I was at your father for letting you join the Army? Do you know how angry I was at you? Do you know how much I worried every day when you were in Iraq? Do you know? Of course you don't know! How could you? You threw away the life I gave you like it was nothing."

"I'm here now," I said.

"What do you have to say to me? Your mother?"

79

"I'm sorry."

"That's not enough. What else do you have to say to me?"

"Ooof," Katie went. I put my arm around her shoulders. She gave me a hard squeeze.

"I love you," I said.

"See? Was that so hard?" She peered up at the ceiling, at the light glowing above her head. All the lights in the house buzzed loudly and became white hot. The soapy waffle iron dropped to the floor. My mother was gone. The lights dimmed back down.

I ran over to the spot where she'd been and dropped to my knees. I felt around, but all that was left of her was a single gray hair that I pinched up off the linoleum and soap suds. I picked up the waffle iron and placed it on the counter. The kitchen was immaculate. I placed the gray hair on the edge of the sink.

My phone chirped in my bedroom. "I'll get it," Katie said. She scurried off and quickly returned with the phone grasped in both her hands. She held it out to me. I took it from her and quickly read the message.

"I'm the night janitor," I said.

"Night janitor," Katie said.

"I'm working tonight."

"Working tonight. Can I come with you?"

"Of course," I said. "You can keep me company if you like."

"Okay," she said. "Will your mother be back?"

"I think so," I said. "I'm not so sure about my father."

"We'd better go see him then," Katie said.

"I thought you didn't like him."

"I can always run away."

"Please don't run away. I get worried."

"Okay. I won't. Is there anything to eat here? I'm starving." She made a face. "I don't like your father's icky waffles."

I checked my phone. It was two in the afternoon. "Let's walk down to the tavern. Joe makes a pretty good cheeseburger. He'll let me run a tab."

"I like cheeseburgers," Katie said enthusiastically. She hopped up and down a bit. She walked over to the door and looked back at me. "What are we waiting for? Let's go!"

I opened the door and she sprinted outside, all the way down to the street. I shouted, "Katie, stop!" She stopped. She sprinted back to me.

"You're slow," she said. "Let's go." She took my hand and pulled me along. A few doors down, she let go of my hand and ran up to a tree. She caressed the trunk, and ran back to me. "I know a few others in this neighbor. I've been here before. Some are nice. Some aren't." She took my hand again and pulled me. "C'mon, c'mon, slowpoke. Cheeseburger!"

I heard a car puttering up alongside us. It was a tan Plymouth with tiny pockmarks of rust dotting the lower extremities of the vehicle. The AM radio played a tinny version of Elton John's "Tiny Dancer." The driver's side window was rolled down. Patty McGinty was the driver. "Need a ride?" she asked, slowing way down.

"No," I said. "We're good."

"Come on, Phil. Hop in. We barely had a second to talk last night. I want to see how you're doing. Your stray can come along with you."

"She's not a stray," I said. "Not anymore."

"No arguments," Patty said, bringing the vehicle to a squealing stop. Her brakes needed some work by the sound of it. "Get in."

I walked over to the car and opened up the back door for Katie. She quickly slid to the center of the back bench seat. I shut the door and walked around the back of the vehicle. I got in the passenger seat beside Patty. Katie hung her head over the back of the front seat. She was slightly out of breath from all the running around she'd been doing.

"Where you headed?" Patty asked.

"Joe's," I said.

"Got a craving for a cheeseburger, huh?"

"Care to join us?" I asked.

"Nah. I got shopping to do."

"So," I went, not knowing what else to say. She was physically pretty, but my crush on her was a long time gone. I didn't find her all that interesting. I pulled out my phone and checked my messages. Nothing.

"I heard you got married," Patty said. "Out in Chicago."

"Yes. Married and divorced. I have a beautiful daughter. Her name's Annie."

"Annie?" Katie said, angrily. "You named your daughter Annie?"

"Yes," I said. "I named her Annie."

"Why?"

"I don't know," I said. I reached back into my memory. It was blank. For a moment, it was so blank, I couldn't see Annie's face. I couldn't remember what my ex-wife looked like. What was her name? "I don't know. Is it important?" My heart raced.

"Yes, it's important. It's very important. Wait? Are you okay?" I was hyperventilating. Katie reached over the seat and grasped my earlobe. I almost immediately calmed down. "You're pretty," Katie said to Patty, changing the subject. She glanced back at me momentarily, looking worried.

Patty was oblivious. "Thanks. I've seen you around. What's your name?"

"I'm Katie. Do you have any water?"

"We'll be there in a minute," I told Katie, catching my breath. How'd she do that? How'd she calm me down so quickly? "Joe has water for you."

"Okay," Katie said. "Take deep breaths." It was like she'd calmed me down like this a million times before.

"Yes. Thank you. I am." I took a deep breath to demonstrate.

"Did you see that snow this morning?" Patty asked.

"I rolled around in it," Katie said.

"Of course you did," Patty said. "These strays. They're more dog than human, even when they're human."

"I have a graveyard shift job," I said. "I was asleep during the snow."

"Katie had enough fun for the both of you," Patty said. She reached around and scratched the side of Katie's head. Katie closed her eyes for a moment, enjoying the attention, and then opened them and looked at Patty adoringly. "She's a sweetheart."

"Phil doesn't remember me," Katie said.

"Yeah, but honey. The way he looks at you. Something's going on. I think Phil remembers me, but he just doesn't care. He used to have a crush on me, but now he looks at me differently," Patty said. "Here we are." She pulled up to the curb in front of the tavern. A group of men sat on the curb, their hands clasped in front of them. They all wore pearl-button Western shirts, jeans and work boots. Their hair was neatly trimmed. The ones that had facial hair had that neatly groomed as well. "Ignore those guys," Patty said. "Just walk past them."

"Thanks for the ride, Patty," I said, opening the door and getting out.

"No problem," she said.

I opened the back door, and Katie bounded out. She saw the group and backed up a bit.

Patty drove off, leaving us there with the gang.

A short man stood up. He was five feet five, maybe six, but carried himself like someone who was much larger. "Hey, mister," he said to me. "You got a couple of bucks? For a drink?" I recognized him from the flyer that the police had given me.

"No," I said.

"Then whatcha doing here?" He looked around me. "Hey, is that Katie? Whatchoo doing here, girl? You find a home with this guy?"

"I don't have to talk to you," Katie said.

The other men and boys stood up. Two of them appeared to be in their sixties, or even older. The rest of the dozen or so men were in their twenties.

"Don't be that way," the little man said. "Don't be so cold."

"Can we go inside?" Katie asked me.

"Are you guys going to be trouble?" I asked the little man.

"No, no. No trouble. We ain't gonna be trouble, are we fellas?" he said, turning his head slightly.

All of the men were standing. They pretended to confer with each other. "No way," one of the two older men said. "We're standup citizens. We're not no strays. Not like some." They laughed and bumped chests.

"See, mister. It's like that," the little man said, grinning toothily.

The other older man pulled out a hand-painted cardboard sign. It said, in bright red capital letters, NEEDS WORK. "You know anyone who's hiring?" the man called over to me.

"Buy and Bye," I said.

"Buy and Bye, you say? He say, 'Buy and Bye' is hiring," one older man said to the other.

"Shit, then you can toss out that sign," the other one said. They laughed.

"We need a drink," the little man said. "Maybe not all of us. But some of us. You got a ten on you? Maybe a twenty? Or you know someone who maybe needs lawn work? Where you going, Katie? You gonna run away or something?" He leaned closer to me and winked. "She's always running away, mister. That's why she's a stray. Us? We ain't strays. We ain't going nowhere."

Joe Ziska banged through the front door of the tavern, a bucket of water in his hands. They spun their heads around and in a blink, I was standing amongst a pack of wild dogs, led by a chihuahua. "Get the fuck out of here!" Joe shouted. He doused the chihuahua at my feet, who shook and ran along with the rest of them.

I turned and scanned around for Katie. She was at the far edge of the parking lot, her arms wrapped around herself, shaking a bit. I walked over to her and touched her arm. She calmed down. "I was scared," she said.

"It's okay. We'll go inside. I'll tell Joe he can trust you."

"Okay," she said. She stopped hugging herself and threw her arms around me. I felt her stop shivering. There were feelings welling up. Old feelings. I took her hand and led her over to Joe.

"This is Katie," I said.

"She's a stray. She used to hang out with those other strays," Joe said.

"She's with me."

"I don't like strays hanging around here. It's bad for business."

"She's with me."

"All right. She's with you," Joe said. "You both look hungry. Maybe you'd like a cheeseburger? What about you, young lady?"

"I'd like a cheeseburger," she said uncertainly.

Joe set down the bucket next to the door. "Then you'd better get inside."

We sat at a small round table near the men's room. We watched Frank drinking at the bar. Then we watched him get up and stumble to the men's room, right past us.

Joe brought out the cheeseburgers. He brought me a Black Label and Katie a glass of iced tap water. Katie gobbled down the cheeseburger in four or five bites, barely chewing it. She gulped down the water. She sucked on her greasy fingers afterward, and stared greedily at the remaining half of my cheeseburger. I gave it to her. She took a bit more time eating it. When she was almost done, Frank came stumbling out of the washroom and stopped at our table. He waited for Katie to finish and patted her on the head. "What's your name?" he asked her.

She licked her thumb. "Katie."

"That's a pretty name. Where'd you find her?" he asked me.

"She found me," I said. "She saved me from some tramps."

"The blood stealing tramps? I heard about them," Frank said. I glanced down for a moment. Frank had pissed all of the front of his trousers.

Katie licked each digit on both hands.

"Are you still hungry?" I asked her.

"I'm full. Maybe we should go visit your father now? I know where he is," she said.

"I do, too," I said.

I wanted to get out of there before the pack of strays showed up again.

"I'll put it on your tab!" Joe shouted from the bar. He was working on the same glass as the day before. "Pay up at the end of the month."

"Sounds good, Joe."

The beer had done me a world of good. The sun was bright walking down the road. Katie sprinted ahead of me, and then slowed down waiting for me to catch up. I caught her hand. "Katie, did you see my mother today?"

"That's a silly question."

"Yes or no?"

"Yes. I saw her. Then she disappeared. It happened." I let go of her hand. She ran around in someone's yard with a beagle. They rolled in the grass together, and then Katie was a dog again. She trotted alongside me, panting.

Soon enough, we were at the house where my father was working. He was driving stakes in the ground around the circumference of the yard. He'd dug an indentation into the ground already.

"Dad, are you sure you should be working this hard?" I asked him. He'd made a lot of progress for a day's work.

"I'm fine. I see you still have that stray hanging around with you."

"Yes."

He stood up and groaned, stretching his destroyed back. "Jesus H. Christ. The spirit is willing. The body revolts." He was all blurry and translucent for a moment, and then slowly came back into focus.

"I'm worried about you."

"Stop being worried."

"I can't help it."

"Of course you can. What kind of man can't turn off his worry? When you were overseas? I didn't worry for a second. I knew you'd pull through. Your mother? She cried every goddamned day."

"I know."

"You shouldn't have called her so much."

"I needed to hear her voice," I said. "I was seventeen. I was still a child. I needed my mother."

"You could have come home while she was dying. Chicago is only six hours away."

"I know. But… I couldn't."

Katie walked up to me, fully human again, and took my hand. She was dressed in jeans, boots and a Bikini Kill t-shirt. "You shouldn't have been mean to Omar," she said, glaring at my father.

"Who the fuck are you again? Oh, that's right. You're a stray. You can fuck right off as far as I'm concerned."

"Just because you're hurt, doesn't mean you get to be mean to everyone," Katie said, squeezing my hand tightly.

A police cruiser drove past, slowing way down in front of us. Then the flashers atop the vehicle turned on and the siren went off, startling Katie. She hid behind me and put her arms around me. The cruiser sped off.

"You're fine," my father said dismissively.

Katie let go and walked around me. She pointed her finger at my father. "Stop being mean."

"We saw mom today," I said.

"The fuck you did," my father said.

"She cleaned the kitchen," I said. "The waffle iron."

"That sounds like your mother." He sighed. He held his lower back with both hands and tilted his head back. "I'm so tired. Why does life have to be like this?"

Katie crept over to him cautiously. She quietly, almost imperceptibly, placed her arms around him. Soon, the two of them were hugging it out. They slowly let go of each other and Katie backed up. He and Katie stood regarding each other. My father wouldn't look at me. He kept his eyes on Katie. "Do you think she'll be back? Your mother?"

"I don't know," I said.

"You can stay," my father said to Katie. "Just don't make a mess in the backyard. Don't dig around."

"Okay," she said.

"I mean it."

"Okay."

"Now get the hell out of here. Both of you. I have work to do."

WE ARE THE DREAMER

The sun dropped into the west, but my father did not return home. Katie and I sat watching TV. The Cavs were on. They were plowing through another opponent in the NBA playoffs. LeBron looked godlike. Flashbulbs exploded every time the ball came to him. And every time it did, it went into the basket.

Katie fell asleep, curled up on the rug. She kicked and yipped. Maybe she was chasing a rabbit in her dream. I thought about how pleasant a dog's dreams must be.

I looked up at the clock and realized that I'd have to go to work. I woke up Katie and she leapt onto the sofa with me. "I have to go to work. Will you be okay here? Dad isn't home. I don't know where he is. Maybe he's still working. He shouldn't be."

Katie clicked over to being human and said, "I'm coming with you. To work."

"You don't have to."

"You need me." She had on jeans and a denim jacket with patches all over it. She wore a Ms. Marvel t-shirt underneath the jacket. She had on faux suede boots. "Let's go."

I put on a jacket I found in my closet, a blue cloth jacket, zippered in the front, with a collar. I think I'd bought it in a thrift store back in high school, back when I was trying out different looks, figuring out who I was.

Katie followed me around the house and then out to the motorcycle. I made her put on the helmet. I kicked it over and she got on the back after I sat down. We rode off into the jet black night on the noisy beast of a cycle. It had its own personality. It was surly and flatulent.

Lights on poles glowed brighter as we rode past, illuminating the potholes, which were wide mouths with no teeth. In the large pothole where we'd found the car, we instead found neat red bricks lining the hole, perfectly placed, evenly spaced.

A man in an Ohio Department of Transportation uniform stood beside the hole, beaming at us, at me, as we blatted past. He raised up three fingers to his brow and gave me the guild salute, and then bowed. I pulled back harder on the throttle and gunned past, the engine vibrating heavily between my knees.

We pulled into the parking lot, now empty, now poorly lit, and I killed the engine. Katie took off the helmet, set it on the motorcycle seat and clicked over to being a dog again. She had on a doggie sweater, blue with white piping. Stitched in cursive on either side was one word: "Comfort." Katie followed me to the door.

Astrid Sogaard was there to meet me. "Is this your dog? Do you need her to be with you? We make accommodations. It's part of our corporate creed. It's written into this company's DNA. We support veterans. We support you. Come inside. May I pet her? She's soft. Aren't you pretty? You're a pretty girl, aren't you? Would she like a treat? I happen to have a nice cookie for her right behind the counter here. C'mere, girl. Come get your treat. Aw! Isn't she precious? Anyhoo, we'll be locking you in overnight. Not much to this job, really. All you have to do is empty out all the wastebaskets into this rolling trashcan, thus consolidating all our trash into one receptacle. Don't worry! It's bigger than it looks at first glance. Don't worry about mopping any of the floors on the sales floor. Swagger, the janitor bot, will take care of them. Give them a big Buy and Bye hello, Swagger. 'Beep, beep' indeed! Ah, Swagger has been a trusted team member since 2015. I know that's only a year, but a year is a long time for our employees. Sadly, most of them don't last even six months. Confidentially, I think that most of the people who take jobs here don't plan on staying. But I've been here since nineteen-ninety-seven. Look at my fifteen-year pin. Isn't that something? Not a lot of people stay at a job nearly twenty years. Just one more to go and I get my twenty-year pin. Then me and my boys will go to the Grand Canyon to celebrate. Their father doesn't get to have all the fun with them. And why should he? He's a layabout. A bum! Uses his time in the service as an excuse for not doing work. Him and his Latin charm. Oh, listen to me natter. I'm not usually this talkative, but it's been, let's say, a challenging evening. That gets me to your one big assignment overnight. I need you to mop out the women's washroom. There was an incident involving plastic packaging and a knife and a shoplifter. The shoplifter cut open a package containing a USB drive and cut his hand. What was he doing in the women's washroom? You tell me. Now there's blood all over the place. It's disappointing. I'm disappointed in people, mostly. They do things that are counterproductive, and not just for Buy and Bye. But for themselves! They do these things and think they should be able to get away with them, but they don't, because crime is for criminals and criminals always get caught because, let's face it, they're not all that bright. If they were bright, they would have normal jobs and not be criminals. Am I right? Of course I am! Oh, silly me. Here's your badge. Place it around your neck and Swagger won't try to mop you up. Let me get a nice little badge for your doggie. Come here, sweetie doggie! I won't bite. Here, let me put this on you. Gimme a little kiss, pretty doggie, right here on my cheek. Oh, she's a good girl. Yes, she is! You won't need any keys. Your badge will get you into every authorized area. If the place catches fire, and it hasn't since I started work here, but if it does catch fire, press the red button next to the front door and you'll be able to get out in a jiffy. Do you have any questions before you start? Oh, right! Where's the cleaning materials? Come with me. Come, come. Here they are, right in here. That's where they are. All of them. I think that's it. I need to get out of here because the auto lock is about to engage and then you'll be stuck in here with me all night, and wouldn't that be a drag? Have a nice night. You, too, doggie! And don't forget about the blood in the women's washroom. It's pretty sticky by now. You'll need some 'Gray Cell Green,' which is in the closet I showed you. That'll get that blood right up. You'll see."

Astrid Sogaard stepped through the front door, turned and waved at me, and the gate slammed down, locking us in for the night.

Katie stood beside me, watching her go. She became human for a minute.

"Do you mind when people treat you like that?"

"Like what? Being condescending?"

"Yeah, like that."

"Not when I'm a dog. Nothing like that bothers me when I'm a dog. I only notice that she's trying to be nice." She reverted to being a dog and trotted away.

I wandered the store for a while, pushing around the little plastic dumpster on wheels. I found wastebaskets and emptied them. It was pleasant. Swagger lumbered around, buffing the floors, humming to himself. Katie found a couch to make herself at home on. She snoozed.

I went into the employee break room and bought a can of Vernor's Ginger Ale out of a machine. I took off my jacket and hung it over the back of a chair. I bought a bag of ketchup-flavored potato chips out of another machine and ate that. I sipped my Vernor's. My mind wandered. I remembered my task.

First, I checked the men's room. It was clean enough. I cleaned the sinks and the three toilets anyway. I mopped the floor with the Gray Cell Green cleaning fluid. The mop was brand-new. I had a soldier's appreciation for a new mop. After I finished, I stood admiring my work. I never had this sense of satisfaction when I sold commodities. The money was good, though.

I took a deep breath and went into the women's washroom. To my surprise, there wasn't much to the puddle of blood. It was maybe ten centimeters in diameter, mostly pink. I went back into the custodian's room and found a package of paper towels, a clear garbage bag and a pair of blue latex gloves. I wiped up the blood using a circular motion and tossed the bloody paper towels into the clear bag. But it wasn't wiping up well. I pulled out a couple more paper towels and wiped. I was merely smearing the blood around, it seemed. I wiped some more. And more. I stood up. The blood was covering a space about a meter in diameter now. The center of the puddle was about a centimeter deep. I looked in my clear bag and it was filled with bloody paper towels. It looked like I was mopping up a crime scene. "Where's all this blood coming from?" I asked aloud.

I stood up and grabbed the mop. I sprayed the area down with Gray Cell Green from a squirt bottle and then mopped the area. It spread out to two meters. The center of the puddle was dark red and the blood was beginning to thicken. I absently scratched my chest and realized that my shirt was bloody. I thought that the blood must have somehow splashed onto my shirt. "Great," I said aloud. "Just fucking great." I thought about taking off my shirt, but I'm too self-conscious about my body to remove an article of clothing in a public place, even if that public place is on lockdown. The blood was oozing down my shirt, wicking its way to my pants. I mopped harder and the blood splashed up against the wall.

Built into the wall was a massive vent. It was a louvered vent about half the size of a house door. It was fastened to the wall by four screws, one in each corner. Blood was dripping out of the vent. I thought that it must be the source of the blood. Maybe something died in there. Maybe something was alive in there. It could be a dog. I was certain that Katie was out in the furniture section, snoozing on a couch, so it wasn't her. But I'm one of those people who gets more upset when a dog dies in a movie than when people do. My imagined dog was bothering me, so I hurried to the custodian's closet and found a tool box. I took out a regular screwdriver and a Phillip's head and brought them back. The vent screws were Phillip's heads, so I tossed aside the other screwdriver and had the vent off quickly. I leaned it up against the wall. I put the screws in that little extra pocket above the right hand pocket of my jeans. The blood soaked my t-shirt now all the way from the collar to the waist, and almost all the way around to my kidneys. It dripped off my scalp and forehead, too. I was sopping wet with blood. I had a mission. I needed to find my hypothetical dog. I crawled into the vent.

I was about ten meters in when I realized that I couldn't see anything anymore. "Hello!" I called out ahead of me. I took out my phone and used it as a flashlight. Dust motes floated. Sugary sand ground into my hands as I crawled.

I came to the end of the vent. I pushed the sheet metal ahead of me gently, testing it. It fell down and slapped onto desert sand. I stepped out of the vent and realized almost instantly where I was. I turned around and the vent was gone. "Shit," I said aloud, panicked. "This isn't where I wanted to go."

I realized that I was in uniform. I had on my armored vest and kevlar helmet. I wore tinted goggles. I held onto my rusty M16A2. My stomach dropped.

Another soldier was standing beside me.

It was like one-hundred-and-ten, but I wasn't sweating. Not yet. I'd barely arrived.

It was PFC Tanaka, the soldier who never took off her gear. She smiled shyly at me. She took off her goggles and stared at me. One brown eye and one blue eye.

"Katie?" I went, gasping. "Katie, is that you? You're PFC Tanaka?"

"It's me. I will always be here, dreaming beside you, Derleth. Um, Phil. Shh. Watch," PFC Tanaka said, pointing.

Out in the desert, obscured in a heat shimmer, a convoy of vehicles trundled along.

"How did I forget you? How could I not know you? You were in my squad."

"You forgot a lot of things. Your head got hurt. It happens. You see me now, though, don't you? I'm right here."

"Yes, I see you."

"Because you refused to see me when we were out here, even before your head got hurt. You refused."

"I'm sorry."

"Shh! Watch, this is the part where you save me. Right here. This part. It's my favorite part. The part where you save me. I don't like what you did immediately afterward. That was pretty stupid."

We watched a little group of boys, teenagers, pop up out of a hidey-hole they'd made in the desert using a board covered with sand. They had an old Soviet rocket launcher. It shouldn't have worked. Pop and no kick. But it fired and Katie and I stood there about twenty-five meters behind the three boys, and about fifty meters from the deuce-and-a-half with the fifty cal mounted on it. And there, on the deuce, was Scabby. And there was PFC Tanaka with all her gear on, fifty meters away.

I watched the boy who wanted to be an artist fly up out of nowhere and push PFC Tanaka down and then shoulder SGT Crabby out of the way. The boy who wanted to be an artist tried to catch the rocket with his hands, like he was trying to catch a wobbly pass in the end zone. The rocket hit him square in the chest and ricocheted up off his head and went up and up and exploded high above. Bam!

We watched PFC Tanaka scramble to her feet and grab the fifty cal. She fired at the three boys and they became puffs of red smoke and bits of red meat.

"That's my least favorite part," Katie said, "but it's the part that I keep seeing."

"Where are you right now?" I asked her.

"I'm asleep on the sofa that's on sale. Only five-hundred-nineteen-ninety-nine."

"But where are we?"

"I'm dreaming. So are you. You're dreaming. We both are. We're dreaming together. It's not the first time. We used to dream together in the desert. It kept us sane. Do you remember now? Please say you remember."

"This feels real." I threw my defective M16 to the ground. The two of us walked over to the boys. They were very much dead. They were reduced to parts. Blood soaked the sand around them for meters around.

"I came to Cleveland to look for you when I got out. I remembered it from the dreams we shared. But you weren't around." Katie got defensive. "I wasn't just waiting around for you. I couldn't go home. I fell into a life." She pointed behind us. "Go back the way you came in."

But there wasn't an exit. "There's nothing there."

"Go look. I'll stand watch here."

I walked back to where I'd entered and tripped over a door handle. I dropped to my hands and knees and wiped away the sand, revealing a half-sized wooden door. "Katie!" I called out, but she was gone. So was the convoy. So were the remains of the boys. I wasn't in uniform anymore. I opened the door and slipped into the vacant space and dropped once again to my knees. I crawled toward florescent lighting in the distance.

At the other end, I emerged into the women's washroom again. The blood on my shirt had dried. I understood now. It was my blood. I reached up to my head and let my fingers gingerly trace the long, crisscrossed scars on my forehead and scalp. I pulled my shirt up and looked at the scars twisting and turning along my sternum like a road map. I pulled my shirt back down. How hadn't I noticed these things?

The blood on the floor was barely there. I mopped a bit and it was all gone. Good as new.

I put the vent back on the wall. It was barely a foot square. All of the little screws were still in my pocket. My hands shook, so it was hard work, but I finally got the cover back on the vent.

I opened the washroom door and Katie was standing on the other side, fully human, staring at me. "So now you know," she said. Her voice was different. She was different. She was more person than dog now.

"Now I know."

"And you can see me again."

"Yes, I can see you. I know who you are. You're my best friend."

"And best friends don't abandon each other."

"I didn't know. I'm sorry. I forgot."

"I know that. Buy me some chips and a Coke and we'll call it even."

"Okay."

"And then I want you to draw me. Just like you did that one time at Forward Operating Base Eagle, when we were fobbits, hanging out." She reached into her pocket and pulled out a folded piece of paper. She unfolded it. It was a sketch of her that I had drawn. In it, she had on all her gear. Like always.

I held it in my shaking hands. It was old and creased. The pencil lines had smeared a bit. I gave it back to her.

"You forgot so much. They didn't do a good job patching you together, did they? They left things out. Important things." She folded up the piece of paper and stuck it back in her pocket.

"Maybe I'm the one who left things out. Maybe because they were important."

"Maybe," she said. "I leave out things, too, sometimes. Important things. Things I don't want to face."

"Like what?"

"Like… stuff. Look, we're talking about you. Making you better. You have to draw again."

"I can't draw anymore."

"You can."

"No. My hands. They shake."

"They're fine. You're fine. We'll find a pencil and some paper. That's all you need to start. You'll draw our dreams. We talked about this back then. You can do it."

"I can't."

"We'll see. I'm not going anywhere. I'm here for the duration." Katie smacked her lips. "I need chips and a Coke. Let's go raid that break room."

Katie and I hung out in the break room. We sat across from each other. We told corny old jokes that our fathers had taught us. Katie told me what it was like being a dog. "It's a lifestyle choice."

"Could I be one?"

"No. I don't think so. It's a matter of disposition. You're too uptight." She reached over and took my hand. "It's okay. It's not for everyone." She ate her own chips and then finished mine. "Ketchup. Ew." She ate them anyway and tapped the crumbs out of the bottom of the bag into her mouth. She washed them down with her can of Coke.

"Katie. What we saw out there."

"In a dream."

"In a dream. Was it real? Was that really us?"

"It was real. That was really us. Sometimes, I go months without seeing it. Sometimes, I see it every night. The shrink at the VA."

"Yeah?"

"He doesn't know everything. He gave me these pills."

"They always give you pills."

"Always. But the pills didn't do much. Then he wanted to talk about it."

"It turns into ashes in your mouth."

"Talk. Talk, talk. Talk. Let's talk about your childhood trauma. Like that has anything to do with anything."

"I'm so tired sometimes."

"Me, too. The best part of being a dog is that I get to live in the moment. No past, no future. Just being alive. When I dream as a dog, it's all goodness."

"That sounds wonderful."

"It is. Kind of. But you give up your autonomy. You need a person who needs you. That's also a dog's life. That kind of sucks."

"Are you really going to stay with me?"

"Now that you're back? Now that you can see me? Yes. I want to stay with you. I want to see this thing through. I want you to be well again."

"And then you'll leave?"

"And then I'll stay some more." She sniffed at the air. "I don't know what I was thinking coming here. I'm from San Pedro. I surf. Your dreams about Cleveland were so vivid. They made me want to be here."

"You can surf in Lake Erie."

"You can do a lot of things in Lake Erie, but you have to watch out for the Toxic Blob."

"They say it's sentient. They say it wants to come home."

"I don't doubt it. It wants to crawl up the water pipe leading into the city. It wants to live inside us all."

"So we can atone for our sins."

Katie giggled. "You're so Catholic."

"I'm sorry."

"Don't be sorry. I like that you're so Catholic. So filled with guilt. Do you know that you used to cross yourself before you burned those big pots of shit?"

"No kidding?"

"No kidding. Like you were praying over everyone's shit. It was sweet in a weird way." She perked up a bit. "Do you think you'd like to go to San Pedro with me some day?"

"How will we get there?"

"We could buy a car. We could hitchhike. We could take a train. I've always wanted to take a train. What do you think?"

"Yes."

"Then it's settled. But first, we have to get you well."

"How do we do that?"

"You have to draw again."

"How long did we know each other?"

"Nine months. You were the only person that made it bearable."

"You never took off your gear."

"I took it off, but only to shower."

"You slept in it."

"I did. I slept in it. I had my reasons. There was a man who…" She shook her head like she was trying to dislodge a memory that had wormed its way in there. "Do you want to walk around the store?"

I put on my coat and zipped it up. The store had grown cold overnight. We got up and walked around the store, past all the merchandise. Katie tried on hats and overcoats. She hung them carefully back up.

We sat down on the cheap couch. The naugahyde groaned underneath us. Katie got up to her knees and traced the scars on my head with her fingers. "I was afraid."

"What were you afraid of?"

"That you were gone. The you inside your head. The one I... you know. That you. Gone."

"You can see my scars?"

"Yes, silly. Can you?"

"I can now."

"Progress. Good progress. Stay here." She got up and bounded through the store. I lost track of her.

Swagger, the janitor bot, rumbled past. He was making a noise that was somewhere between enjoying a beef steak and admiring himself in a mirror. "Hmm. Urm. Ho-ho."

Katie returned with a clipboard and a pencil that wouldn't have looked out of place at a putt-putt golf course. "Here!" she said, handing them to me.

I took them, and looked helplessly at her. "I, uh. I don't know. It's been a long time." I felt a shudder go through my chest and exit through my hands.

My phone chirped in my pocket. I pulled it out. There was a text from Claire. "I don't appreciate your messages!!!"

I typed back, "I'm sorry."

She wrote, "I don't care about your apologies!! I should never have married you."

I didn't know what to say to that. I typed, "I'm sorry."

"That's all you ever say."

"Is Annie okay?"

"Yes. She's fine. She doesn't need you!!! My brother is taking care of us. My father is taking care of us. You don't need to worry about either of us ever again. Read the divorce settlement. Stay away!!!"

"She's my daughter. I worry about her. I want her to be happy."

"If you want her to be happy, stay away from us!!! Stay in Cleveland. It's where you BELONG!!!"

I set the phone aside. It was an unpleasant metal and glass object. More often than not, it made me miserable. It was full of bad news. Or maybe my life was full of bad news. I couldn't tell the difference. I took deep breaths. I tried to find some sort of mystical center. I failed. I picked up the phone again. "Can't I see Annie? Shouldn't she know her father?"

"You know YOUR father!!! What good has it done YOU?!?!"

"If she asks to see me, please let her see me."

"She calls you LOSER DAD!! She hates you!! She won't ask for you. EVER!!!"

"But if she does?"

"STAY AWAY!!! As far as I'm concerned, you should be locked up in a hospital for the rest of your life!!! You're SICK!!! You'll always be SICK!!!"

I realized that Katie was standing behind me, reading over my shoulder. "What did you do?"

"I found out that she was cheating on me with one of the other brokers in my firm. I busted into his house while he was having sex with Claire and smashed everything I could get my hands on. He called the cops. I was hauled away. I ended up in a psych ward at the VA. I'm told I have a panic disorder. Claire and I were divorced six months later. Claire's attorney wrote up the agreement. I signed it in front of a judge. I agreed to everything." I turned around and looked at Katie. Her eyes were brimming with tears. "Combat veteran, he must be nuts. I burned big pots of shit most of the time I was in Iraq. Nobody cares about that. To them, the only thing I did there was the last thing I did there."

"You don't get to see your daughter?"

"No. I don't get to see my daughter. Claire got our savings, the condo in Highland Park. She got exclusive custody. I am a danger to people. Crabby couldn't save me at the firm. I got canned. What could I do? I came home. Here I am. Here I am in O-H-I-O."

"Now it's my turn to say 'I'm sorry.'" She got serious for a moment. "Why did you name her Annie?"

"I don't know."

"You'll remember," Katie said darkly. "Eventually. Then you'll apologize to me."

"Can we save the drawing for another night?" I pushed the clipboard and tiny pencil away from me on the couch.

"Yes. Can you do me a favor?"

"Sure."

"Hand me the phone." I handed it to her. She pushed the button on the side of it and it powered down. She put it in her back pocket. "Fair warning. I may chew on this phone later."

"As part of your lifestyle choice."

She beamed. "Yes. As part of my lifestyle choice."

"I wish I'd known you were here. I wish I'd remembered you earlier."

"Don't wish, Phil. Wishes don't do anything except fester and become resentment. Hope is better. Hope for the best. Don't wish for it. There's a difference." She ran her hand through my hair and touched my forehead scars again. "You can see me. That's enough for now. Progress comes in small steps."

"You sound like a VA shrink."

"I should. I've spent enough time with them. Not all of us have the luxury of external scars. Some of us carry them in hidden places." Katie frowned. "For a few years after I came here, I was more dog than human. I belonged to an old man and I rarely switched back to being human. It's mindless being a dog. You sleep, you eat. You don't worry about anything. You fixate on one person. I followed the old man around the house. He was divorced, never had children. He was good to me. As good as anyone is to a dog. Plus he had every episode of *Farscape* on DVD. I watched them when he left me home alone. I'd phase over to human and eat all his leftovers when he did that, too. Kibble gets old. Take a nice hot bath. Then I'd vacuum the house and change the sheets on his bed because bachelors never do these things. Got sick of a dirty house."

"What happened?"

"He died on the toilet. I watched him die. I switched back to being human. I wept human tears for him. I almost couldn't dial the phone. I almost couldn't speak, it had been so long. I called up nine-one-one and asked for an ambulance. I took some money out of his wallet, he wasn't going to need it, and left."

"I'm sorry."

"I took the money to a restaurant because I wanted to have people serve me, but when people can tell that you're a stray, they treat you worse than a dog. I ate my food, and people were staring and pointing at me. 'Look at that stray. The nerve. Sitting there and eating with decent people.'"

"Jesus."

"It's okay. Everything's okay when I'm a dog. I don't notice those things. I only know that I'm tired or hungry, or I need some affection from my human. I don't think about anything else. I live in the moment, not the past. I don't think about the future either. I certainly don't think about being a soldier." She patted my knee. "And here we are. Back together again. Two amigos."

"I didn't know it, but I missed you all these years. There was an ache inside me that I couldn't define. It seems obvious now."

"Gotta go pee. Think I'll do it on the rug by the front of the store."

"Swagger will take care of it."

She walked away, first on two legs and then on four. Lifestyle choice.

STELLA'S IS OPEN

The auto lock on the front door buzzed and the mesh fence raised back into the ceiling. We watched it, me and my apparent service dog who stood beside me.

Astrid Sogaard said, "Who's the good girl? Who's the best girl? You are! You're such a good girl. Look what I brought for you. Do you like it?" She handed Katie part of a deer antler. Katie carefully took it from her hand and walked a short distance away. "I should have asked you first."

"It's okay."

"I'm so glad. So? Did you clean up in the women's washroom? How did it go? How was the rest of your night? You know you don't have to do much of anything, right? We just want someone to be here. Someone responsible. We know you're responsible, unlike some people I could name. My ex for instance. What a rat. Anyway, you have your schedule. Take a look at it. Four overnights a week, all clumped together so you can have three days off in a row. Isn't that nice? We have another janitor who does the other three. He asked for an extra day off, and the other night janitor quit, so here you are. It's going to be a lovely day outside, don't you think? I'm on salary, so I wouldn't know. Open to close, that's my motto! See you tonight. Don't be late."

I turned around. "Katie?"

She trotted over with the antler in her jaws. I held the front door open for her and she loped out the door. On the other side, she stood up and spat the antler into her hand. She was dressed in shorts and a *Lumberjanes* t-shirt, green basketball shoes on her feet. She handed me the antler. "Put this in your pocket. I'm definitely going to want this later. Let's get on your motorcycle. Vroom, vroom!"

I found a flyer rolled up and sticking in between the throttle cable and the handlebar. I unrolled it and read, "STELLA'S IS OPEN." A black and white rendering of a building shaped like an ice cream cone was under that. Nothing else was on the flyer and nothing else needed to be. "Stella's!" I nearly shouted.

"What's that?" Katie asked, putting on the helmet.

"The best ice cream on earth," I assured her. "And it's right on the lakeshore, on Edgewater Beach. We should hurry. We can be there in twenty minutes. Less if I can get this motorcycle in fourth gear."

"What's the rush?" she asked, tilting her head.

"Stella's is only open three days a year. This could be day three. And she closes her shop the moment she runs out of ice cream."

"I love ice cream," Katie said.

"You should prepare yourself for this ice cream. This isn't an ordinary experience. This goes beyond the normal ice cream experience."

"Okay," she said, like she didn't believe me.

I wanted to say more, but she'd find out soon enough, as long as Stella's ice cream held out.

We hopped on the bike and buzzed our way out to Edgewater Beach, parking a few blocks away due to all the cars clogging the road.

"Damn it," I said, cursing myself for not remembering that Stella's would be open. Why didn't Stella mention it when I was at the Polish buffet?

Katie took off the helmet. It was my turn to grab her hand and drag her along. She giggled at my urgency. We ran alongside each other. When we got close enough to hear the waves lapping on the shore, we had to slow down due to the dozens upon hundreds of twitching humans curled up, alone or in pairs, humming Beatles tunes to themselves, or gurgling, or going, "Ahh, ohh, ahh," in a most contented fashion, their mouths rimmed with chocolate or vanilla. Those were the only two flavors Stella sold. No jimmies, not dipped in anything, and served on a plain cone. One scoop per customer was the rule.

We had to step over Officers Smith and Jones, who were on their backs, each looking like the hand on a clock, their feet meeting at the center of the clock. It was ten until two, according to them. Or maybe twenty until four.

Katie got a little nervous.

"It's okay. They'll be out for about twenty minutes. Maybe half an hour, depending on their tolerance for pure pleasure. Chocolate or vanilla?"

"Vanilla."

"Me, too." I walked up to the window, which was thankfully still open.

Stella leaned out and said, "Is that Phil? We've been seeing a lot of each other lately."

"Yes, ma'am."

"You'll have a vanilla. What about your friend? What's your name, honey?"

"I'm Katie. I'll have a vanilla, too."

"You're a first-timer. You sure you don't want to just take a lick off of Phil's cone?"

"I want the whole experience," Katie said.

Officer Smith muttered, "Mother. Mother!" He twitched.

"Good answer." Stella handed the two cones out. I tried to pay her. "No. You don't have to pay this time, Phil. Say hello to your father for me. He didn't look good the other night."

"I will."

"Take it over to the beach before you taste it. Over that way. Beyond those trees."

I thanked her. Katie and walked across the sand and over to a rocky area beyond the trees, where we could sit and look out on sun-dappled Lake Erie. Little whitecaps formed out on the lake. A red and black hulled freighter was on its way into Cleveland.

"Are you ready?" I asked Katie.

"This had better be good," Katie said, "after all this build-up."

"Go ahead."

She licked it. Her eyes rolled into the back of her head. "Oh. Oh. My. God. Oh." I watched her eat the ice cream and was so enthralled by her reaction that I nearly forgot I had my own. A drip of vanilla on my index knuckle reminded me, and I set into my own ice cream.

I can't even describe how good it is. Words fail.

After we'd finished, we leaned back on the smooth rocks, our heads touching, our eyes closed, wrapt in pleasure beyond mere verbiage. I saw a whirling vortex ahead of me and heard Katie laughing somewhere inside. I ran toward the sound of her laughter and caught up with her. We were on a different beach, this one in California. Katie was in a blue wetsuit, a surfboard under her arm. She was a teenager, untouched by war. We both were. I was in a wetsuit. I knew how to surf, having done so in Lake Erie, but this was altogether different. The waves. They were huge. Out over the Pacific Ocean was the aurora borealis, glowing and sparkling. We ran out into the surf, mindlessly happy, together, best friends on a great adventure. No responsibilities. No job to speak of. Just a couple of kids paddling out to catch a wave. Katie caught one first and she rode it almost all the way to the beach before wiping out. I hopped a wave and for a moment, I was a real surfer and the euphoria was beyond anything I felt in my life, and then I crashed and tumbled and found myself next to Katie looking out over Lake Erie again. We sat up at almost the same time.

"Were you…?" I asked.

"We were in San Pedro. Man, you need some surfing lessons."

"Sounds like you're volunteering."

"You weren't kidding about that ice cream. Can we go back for seconds?"

"No," I said. "That's against the rules. One cone per season."

"Rules suck," Katie said.

"Everyone should get a chance at a cone. It's only fair."

"Bliss." Katie sat up straighter and pointed. "Look." I looked off toward the east. The rising sun turned Cleveland honey-colored. My city glowed. My Cleveland. "Wicked," Katie said, almost in a whisper.

A tall man, taller than even LeBron, walked up to us. He wore an Ohio Department of Transportation uniform—chambray shirt with "OhDOT" stitched above his right pocket, denim trousers, scuffed boots, cockeyed grin. He placed three fingers on his right eyebrow. "Greetings, brother."

I returned his salute. Katie had phased over to being a dog. She sat and stared at the man, a little whine coming out of the back of her throat.

"I've come to have a serious discussion with you. About your father."

"What about dad?"

"He is in violation of several rules of the guild right now. He's worked too many hours in a row. He's split into three workers. He's—"

"What do you mean 'he's split into three workers'?"

"I mean just that, friend. That's in clear violation of guild rules, right there. Along with the hours. And the material he's working with. That is also in violation. He's practically begging to be sanctioned."

"Sanctioned?"

"With extreme prejudice." He turned at glared at Katie. "This stray. Is she yours?"

"She's with me."

"Don't let her get too far away from you. They tend to disappear."

"Are you threatening her?"

"I'm telling you a fact, friend. As one brother to another. You should thank me."

"Okay," I said.

"Go to your father now. Stop him. Stop him, or we will have to stop him. He is a brother in longstanding, otherwise we would have done so already. Brother Chestnut sends his regards." The man turned and walked away. He walked along the beach away from us in his scuffed boots, leaving footprints behind him.

Katie said, "What was that all about?"

"We'd better get to my dad."

"Wait. Wait a second." She cocked her head. She was a dog. She was human. She was a dog again. She was human again. "I can hear her."

"Hear who?"

"Her. The Toxic Blob. She's crying. She's lonely."

"Is she saying something?"

"Yes, but I don't understand the language."

"She should speak English, unless the Canadians corrupted her with French."

"Maybe she doesn't speak a language. Or maybe it's her own language."

"What should we do?"

"Nothing for now, I guess. What can we do?"

"Nothing."

We sat staring into each other's eyes for a long minute. For a moment, I thought about leaning over to kiss her, but that's not something you do to a friend, especially one who's trying to help you become yourself again.

"Katie?"

"Hmm?"

I couldn't formulate what I wanted to say to her. The thought was important, I knew, but it eluded me. Thoughts often did that. I drifted off into a semi-somnolent state. My eyes closed. I heard the seabirds calling out to one another. I heard the surf. I forgot where I was. The rich vanilla ice cream's magic was making everything better. It swirled counterclockwise in my stomach.

"Phil. Wake up." I opened my eyes and Katie's face was the world. Her nose was an inch from mine. Her hand was on my shoulder. She gave me a shake. "I'll be in front. I'll pilot the motorcycle."

"You know how to?"

"I'm from Cali, dude." She smiled at me. "You put on the helmet this time and ride on the back. We have to go visit your dad."

"Right."

"Are you okay?"

"Yes." I meant it, too. I felt more okay now than I had in years. I looked out over the lake. "My marriage, after the first six months, was clearly a sham. Claire knew it. She kept saying, 'I thought I was marrying a soldier. A man.' She liked the colorful ribbons on my chest. The Purple Heart. The Bronze Star. She liked the idea of me, but not the real me. I was barely a soldier. I tried to talk to her, but she didn't want to listen. I told myself and I told her that she was beautiful like sunshine. That I loved her. Then we had the baby, nine months out of the gate, and we stayed together, focussing on the baby. I worked long hours. I told myself I worked long hours because I loved my wife and my child, but work was just a way of avoiding my wife and my child. It was a way of avoiding my memories, which would crowd in on me in quiet moments. I was a functional adult doing functional adult things. I was a husband. I was a commodities broker. I was a man who rode the train to and from work. Busy, busy. Nothing to see here. Move along. My memories of the Army were all stained and jagged. Big pieces were missing. The missing pieces scared me, so I left them wherever they were. Not here. Not with me. The normal wife and the normal child and the normal life would solve everything. Normal, normal, normal." I turned back to Katie. She sat, patiently listening. "Katie, why did I stop seeing you before the, um. Thingie. Before that? What happened? Did I do something wrong? I did something wrong."

"We can talk about that later. There's too much to say. You and I. You and me. We... I don't want to talk about it right now. Can we do that later?"

"Okay."

"You didn't do anything wrong. Okay?"

"Okay."

"You told me you loved me. A few days before the convoy. It kind of freaked me out. I wasn't expecting it."

My heart kicked into high gear. "I'm sorry. I knew I did something wrong. I always do something stupid. Say something stupid." I gasped for air.

"No, no, no." Katie reached over and grasped my earlobe between her thumb and index finger. "Close your eyes." I closed my eyes. She gently held on, applying light pressure. "Shh. Shh." My panic attack quickly subsided. "I don't know how you can be so calm in violent situations and freak out over something like that."

"There's less at stake in violent situations."

"You could get killed."

"It doesn't seem that important what happens to me. Not at the time anyway." My heart slowed down to normal. "I never want you to feel... uncomfortable. Not around me. Not ever. When I care about someone, they're the center of the world." I opened my eyes. Katie let go of my earlobe and looked away. "I can't half-ass friendship. I can't help it."

"I know that. Why do you think I came looking for you after I got out? There were too many things left unsaid. You were so hurt. All that blood. And that look you gave me, when you were on the ground. There was so much blood. All they'd tell me was that you survived golden hour. 'Privacy Act,' they said, when I asked where you were," she said, still not looking at me. "What were you thinking about when you tried to catch that RPG?"

"I don't remember. There's a lot I don't remember."

"Maybe it's best you don't remember that. There are some things that I wish I could forget. Even before the Army. Especially before the Army."

"Like what?"

"Like maybe mind your own business." She smacked herself in the head with the heel of her hand. "Bad girl!" She smiled and glanced over at me. "Sorry. Listen. Do you remember telling me that you loved me?"

"I don't."

"Baby with the bath water."

"I wish—"

"Don't wish. I warned you about that."

"I hope… that I can remember the good things." She peered over at me from the corner of her blue eye. "I remember that you're my best friend."

Katie turned fully toward me and we gazed into each other's eyes. "That's a start. Do you want to give me a hug?" We stood. We hugged. "Good boy," she said, and ruffled my hair.

THE DARKNESS UNDER THE SINK

"Put your hands on my hips," Katie said, straddling the motorcycle. "Anticipate my gear shifts and don't hit me in the back of my head with the helmet."

"Maybe you should wear the helmet," I said, holding it in both hands, standing behind the motorcycle.

"Get on, chicken." She leapt up in the air and stomped down on the kickstarter. The Fuerte roared to life.

Something was different. I stood wondering what it was for a moment, and then I realized: No black smoke. It was quieter, too. It liked Katie more than it liked me, I guessed. I put on the helmet and got on behind Katie, placing my hands on her hips. I felt warm from my proximity to her. She shifted the Fuerte into gear and we zipped away from Edgewater Beach, back toward Kamm's Corners. She navigated the roads expertly. Stray dog's knowledge. We pulled into our driveway. I got off. She pulled the bike around to face the street and said, "Look inside."

I took off the helmet and handed it to her.

I opened the side door gently. One way led to the basement. The other into the kitchen. I could hear some clinking around in there, so I peeked around the corner. My mother, no more than a shade, was washing every glass in the kitchen cabinet. She noticed me staring at her.

"Are you remembering more, sweetie?" she asked, not looking away from her work. She examined a glass, holding it up to the overhead light in the kitchen, studying it for water spots.

"A bit more."

"That's good. I asked for you, when I was dying. I asked, but I knew you wouldn't come, because the real you never came home from the war." I walked over to my old chair. I sat down. "Do you remember? When you came home on leave from the hospital? The one in Illinois. Do you remember that?"

"I came home on leave?"

"Your father picked you up at the airport. You sat right there." She pointed at me, at the table, at my chair, where I'd automatically sat down. "And you said nothing. I looked into your eyes and knew that my boy wasn't around. He was somewhere else. Or he was gone, possibly for good."

"I said nothing?"

"I'm lying. The soldier who was sitting there talked enthusiastically about the business courses he was taking at a community college."

"I remember the business courses. I think I have an associate's degree. It may have burned up with my car. Katie's outside. Do you mind if—"

"Yes, I mind. We're having a conversation. She's a good girl, but this is between you and me. Talk to me. Talk to your mother." She held up another glass for inspection, tsked at it, and dunked it back in the clear water in the sink. She wiped it methodically with a white cloth.

"I don't know what to say," I said.

"Tell me what happened at work last night."

"You don't want to know."

"I already know. Dead people know things, you know."

"If you already know…"

"I want to hear you say it. What did you see?"

I told her about it. About Katie. About the rocket. About the boys Katie killed.

Mom racked the glass, satisfied with its cleanliness. "Who do you think you are? Ozzie Newsome? See? You don't think I pay attention to sports, but your mother knows things. You should have talked to me while I was alive. Have you been watching my stories? Keeping up?"

"No," I said.

"That's something dead people have too many of. Stories. But I still wonder what's going on with my stories. I can't turn on the TV. I tried." She finished another glass. "Almost done." She started to fade.

"Will you be back?"

"I never left," she said.

"Mom. Mom, I don't want to ask this."

"Go ahead. I know what you're going to ask, but you have to say it. It has to come out of your mouth."

"Did it hurt?"

"The bone cancer? Bone pain is the worst pain. You've forgotten about your cracked sternum and your cracked skull, but soon enough, you'll get a reminder. And you'll think of your mother, won't you?"

"I'm sorry, Mom."

"I know you are, sweetie." She put down her final glass and turned to face me. "Your father isn't here. He's still at that house. He never left. You better go get him before the guild does." She walked over to where I was sitting. I stood up. "I'd say 'give me a hug,' but we weren't that kind of family, were we?" She faded completely away.

I cried.

I walked over to the sink and splashed some of the water in there on my face. I unplugged the sink and watched the water swirl down and gurgle and disappear. I wiped my face with a paper towel and blew my nose. I opened the cabinet doors under the sink, intending to throw away the paper towel in the wastepaper basket, but it was black as night under there. I let go of the paper towel and it fluttered and disappeared. I heard a distant noise, like a freight train running through town in the middle of the night. I crouched down and peered in. "Hello," I called into the darkness. My voice echoed back at me as a question. "Hello?" it said.

"Who's there?"

"There?" it echoed.

"Do you need help?"

"Help."

"Should I come down?"

"Come down."

I reached into the blackness. There was nothing there. No wastepaper basket. No pipes. No top. No sides. No bottom. Just blackness. I found a flashlight in a kitchen drawer, turned it on and aimed in into the blackness. The blackness swallowed the light.

Katie grabbed my shoulder and startled me. I dropped the flashlight and it spun as it dropped down and down and down, eventually disappearing. "No," she said. "Not yet. Later."

"Later," her voice echoed.

"I saw my mother again," I said, standing up, closing the cabinet doors.

"I see she cleaned all the glasses. My mother would have done the same thing, if she'd died. She's still alive out in California. She got remarried to a dentist, after my father died."

"What happened to your father?"

"Oh, he just faded away. It happens."

"Like my father."

"No, not like your father. Your father's fighting it." Katie patted me on the chest. "It was when I was in high school. He lost everything in the real estate market. One day, after we were broke, he sat down, and then the next he was half way gone. The day after that, he was a shade. My mother begged him to stay, but he slipped away without a word. We were evicted from our house. It was a pretty nice house in a pretty nice neighborhood. I joined the Army. We talked about this back in the Army, hiding away from everyone else behind the big stacks of conex boxes. We'd sit together during our off-duty time and talk. You were a good listener. That's one of the things I liked about you."

"I'm sorry I don't remember much."

She grabbed my cloth jacket and shook me a bit. "I want you back. The real you."

"I wish—"

"No." She let go of my jacket.

"I hope that I do come back."

"Let's do more than hope. Let's work on it."

"I promise I will."

"And when you're back, the real you, I want to take you to California. You can meet my mother. My stupid little brother, too. I'll teach you how to surf properly."

"I think I'd like that."

"Let's go get your father. I assume he's still out at that house."

"That's what Mom said."

We got back on the motorcycle, me in the rear, and sped over to the house where my father was.

I saw him working on the wall. It was three feet high already. I saw him mixing mortar, too. I saw him sorting bits of stone and other things. I recognized parts of my Mustang in the mix. Pieces of asphalt. Pavers. A collection of shoes. A pair of dentures. I walked over to the version of my father who was sorting through the material. "Dad. What are you doing?"

"Working," he said. "What does it look like I'm doing?"

"Who are those other two?"

"You know who they are, dummy. They're me. Gotta work three times as hard. Gotta get the job done. Another few hours and the wall will be four feet high. That's what the job requires. That's what the client will get."

I glanced over at the house. A man peered through the drapes. He snapped them shut when he saw me looking at him.

"Don't let your stray piss on it."

"She's a girl. Girls squat," I said.

Katie was trotting around. She walked up to one of my fathers and sniffed at him cautiously. He waved her away and she backed off, whining a bit. She walked over to me and put her head under my hand. I absently petted her while talking to my father.

"Dad, you need to stop. The guild is upset with you."

"Big deal. They're toothless."

"They're not toothless, dad. They're serious. They're going to come after you."

"Not me. I'm untouchable."

"What makes you say that?"

"I'm fully lettered. Guild rules say you can't go after a man who's fully lettered. We'll be done quicker if you help out. Grab those shoes and that brake pad and bring it over to me at the wall, and then help me, the one over there, mix that mortar. Another hour and we've got this licked."

"And then you'll be done?"

"Then I'll be done. I'll go home and soak in a hot bath. I'll read the sports section. Did the Cavs win last night?"

"Yes. They're going to the finals."

"Great! Our client is giving me his seats if there's a game seven. He's paying me with his car. Go in the garage and take a look."

I walked over to the garage and peered in. It was a nineteen-sixties Ford Mustang, aquamarine with orange racing stripes. It was a beauty. So much chrome.

I helped my trio of fathers for the next hour, and we quickly finished off the wall together. I was kind of proud that parts of my burned up Mustang ended up in there. All-in-all, it wasn't a bad looking wall, as walls go. I've seen my share having grown up building them.

My father's three personas merged back into one man, as the three of them strode toward the front door of the house, all of them hunched over in pain, their collective backs merging into one sore back as he rang the doorbell.

Katie stood beside me, lightly grasping my arm at the elbow. "Is he done? Are you both done?"

"Yes," I said. "I think it's time to go home and go to sleep."

"Then let's go."

I watched the man hand my father an envelope and a set of keys. My father opened the envelope. He seemed satisfied. The two men shook hands and the door closed.

Katie pulled me over to the motorcycle. I put on the helmet. We rode home, beating my father into the driveway. She parked next to the garage, leaving room for the new car to go up the driveway and into our garage.

We didn't notice that Ohio Deputy Undersecretary of Transportation Merle Chestnut was standing in the backyard, next to the birdbath with the bubbling black liquid in it. He was dressed in the uniform of an OhDOT employee, complete with scuffed boots. I took off my helmet and stared over at him, sure that he was an aberration of some sort. A glitch. "Hello?" I went. "Hello?"

"We asked you nicely, as a brother, to do us a favor. But instead of stopping your father, you joined in. There are consequences for such behavior." He dunked his thumb in the bubbling dark liquid and held up his blackened thumb, almost like he was approving of us. He wasn't. He walked over to us and said, "Remember that you brought this on yourself." He stuck his thumb on Katie's forehead, leaving a thumbprint behind, like she'd gone to Ash Wednesday. She backed away from him, startled. "Poor. Little. Doggy," he said deliberately, enunciating each syllable.

The 1970 AMC Rambler station wagon quickly pulled into the driveway. We stood there, mouths agape, speechless. Ohio Deputy Undersecretary of Transportation Merle Chestnut opened the back door of the Rambler, slid into the car, the door slammed shut, and the Rambler backed quickly out of the driveway and into the street, roaring away.

My father pulled into the driveway in the cherry Mustang a minute later. He shut down the engine and got out of the car. He walked around it, patting it appreciatively. "She's a beauty," he said. "What a great deal." He finally noticed the two of us standing there. He walked over to Katie. "Where'd you get that smudge on your head?"

"It was Chestnut," I said.

"What did he say?" my father asked, angrily.

I told my father what he'd said.

"He said it like that? 'Poor. Little. Doggy?'"

"Yeah," Katie said nervously.

"Shit. You have to stay inside until further notice. No outdoors for you," my father told Katie. "That guy's serious. He's a dog killer."

"Dad." I put my arm around Katie automatically.

"How do you think Omar ended up dead? You think that was an accident? He had people waiting for Omar to come outside. He assassinated that dog. I told Marie not to let him out, but your fucking uncle had to come over."

"Are you saying that Merle Chestnut killed my dog? And that he's going to kill Katie?"

"He's going to kill this girl when she's a dog. Yes." My father pulled a rag out of his pocket and wiped Katie's head clean. "That's the dark secret of the guild. They kill dogs. They're dog killers. That's how they keep people in line. I leaked it to a guy I know from the *Plain Dealer*, and I've been on Merle Chestnut's shit list ever since."

"What the hell?" I went.

"He knows that killing a dog is easier than killing a person. No consequences. Not legally. But it hurts just as much. You think I didn't miss Omar? I loved that little shit."

"And you let me join that guild without telling me?"

"It seemed like a good idea at the time."

"You're a goddamned idiot, Larry," I said, using my father's first name for the first time in my life. "I ought to knock you on your ass."

"Jesus H. Christ," my father said. "It's about time you did."

I let go of Katie and slugged him. He dropped to the ground like a sack of potatoes. "Stay down for a minute."

"I can't get up, so easy ask." He adjusted his jaw and blinked.

I grasped Katie by the shoulders and turned her toward me. "We have to get you on a bus. Or a train. Send you far away. Send you home. You can't stay. That guy's gonna have you killed."

"I'm not going anywhere," Katie said. "I don't have to be a dog when I'm outside. I can be an inside dog. I only really need to be a dog when I'm asleep, so I don't have human dreams."

"Don't go outside period," my father said from the ground.

"Shut the fuck up, Larry," I said, pointing over at him. "Stay down."

"Yes, sir," my father said. He arched an eyebrow at my insolence.

I turned my full attention to Katie. "Katie, I won't let you die."

"I'm fine. I'll be fine. I just have to resist the urge to flip over to canine. It'll be fine. I'm not leaving you. I'm here for the duration, remember?"

"I won't hold you to that promise if it means losing you."

"I'm staying. End of discussion." We hugged. She kissed me on the cheek afterward. "This is you. You're getting closer."

My father piped in. "Aw. That's sweet. One of you dummies want to help me up?" I walked over to him and reached down. My father reached up and grabbed my hand. I pulled him to his feet, eliciting a painful groan from him. "My fucking back. Sweet baby Jesus." He looked at us guiltily. "Let's get inside. Inside is good."

The radio in the garage clicked on and serenaded us into the house with, "Oh, ho, ho, it's magic... you know! Never believe, it's not so!"

"I hate that stupid radio," my father muttered. "Gonna toss that sucker out. First thing tomorrow."

Katie and I each grabbed an arm and helped him up the steps to the side door of the house. We took him through the kitchen and into the living room and set him on the shabby sofa. He groaned and leaned back. "Get me some whiskey. Please, son." I went into the master bath and dug some pills out of the cabinet above the sink. I brought them out to him. He shook the amber vial and said, "I think these are illegal now. Got these on a trip to Mexico." He dry swallowed two and handed me the vial. I took the rest back into his bathroom.

Katie brought over the ottoman and placed it under his feet. She took off his work boots and placed them near the front door. His socks were shot full of holes and filthy. A big toe jutted out through a hole. The toenail was cracked and yellow.

"You stay inside, okay," he said to her. "You stay here. Don't go out. OhDOT has people everywhere where there are potholes in Ohio, and that's everywhere." He turned his head toward the kitchen. "Marie! Marie, are you around? Goddamnit, Marie! Sound off if you're here."

No answer was received.

"I saw the glasses, Marie. Is that some sort of commentary on my cleaning skills? The glasses are clean. They don't have to be perfect."

No answer was received.

"Jesus H. Christ," my father muttered. "She might as well be here. Same, same." My father faded for a moment, went out of focus, buzzed, and then snapped back into complete existence.

"That's it. I'm calling a doctor." I went into the kitchen, dialed directory assistance and they connected me with the Cleveland Clinic. After going through several prompts, I finally ended up talking to a telephonic medical practitioner.

He had me describe my father's symptoms, occasionally prompting me forward with, "Uh-huh" and "mmm-hmm" and "interesting." "Mister Derleth, I'm going to be frank with you. There's plenty of this going about. Your father suffers from what we call 'Metaphysical Adjustment Disorder,' or MAD. He requires someone with a different doctorate than mine: A Ph.D. in Philosophy." He gave me the number for the Ohio State University's Philosophy Department. "For God's sake, don't take him to an empiricist. He'll dissipate within minutes. You'll have to drive him down to Columbus for a consultation, I'm sure. Philosophers don't travel well, unless there's a conference that features salted peanuts in the shell. I find that philosophers will do anything if you pay them with peanuts."

I called the number and was transferred over to an associate professor who was coming to a conference in Cleveland for the International Philosophical Association Fall Workshop on Socio-Environmental Asymmetrical Ethics and Subjectivities. He told me to call him "Doctor Bertie." Doctor Bertie said he'd be happy to "swing by" either before or after the conference. "Um, I hate to bring this up. But there's the matter of... um, uh..."

"I will have a bushel basket of salted peanuts in the shell waiting for you," I said.

"Splendid!" he chirped. I gave him our address and he hung up.

I walked past my father and he was fast asleep on the couch, still corporeal. Still opaque.

I followed Katic into the bedroom. She flipped over to being a dog. She chewed on her deer antler on the bed. I went into my bathroom, stripped off my clothes and took a long hot shower. I toweled off and walked back into the bedroom. She was fast asleep on the foot of the bed, the deer antler on the floor. I stared at the antler and watched as it phased into a copy of Marjane Satrapi's *Persepolis*. "Always wanted to read that one," I muttered. I slipped into bed as quietly as I could. She was yipping a bit in her sleep, her paws twitching. I pulled down the shade and drifted into a deep, shared sleep.

FUN BOSS TODD

In my dream, I stood outside of the apartment I'd shared with my wife and daughter. It was the middle of the night. I saw them up in the window, silhouetted there by lamplight. Claire was combing out Annie's long, brown hair. Annie let out little cries. "Be still!" Claire said sharply. "Stand still. Stop fidgeting."

"I shouldn't be standing here," I said aloud.

"No, you shouldn't!" David Lynch said. He was the young David Lynch, the one who directed *Blue Velvet*. His hair was all slicked back like a Roaring Twenties gangster. He was smoking a cigarette, leaning on a lamppost. "I'm here to remind you that this is a merely a dream."

"Thanks," I said.

"You can stare all you want in a dream," David Lynch said loudly, gesturing toward the window. "It doesn't matter. Stare all you want."

"I guess I'm trying to work something out," I said.

"Yes!" David Lynch said. "That's fairly obvious. You don't need me to point that out to you. Say! Would you like to go get some coffee and a milkshake with me? I'll introduce you to Isabella Rossellini."

"Boy, would I. But every time I take you up on your offer, something goes horribly wrong."

"Right! The man throwing a urinal out of the window and hitting you on the head." David Lynch smiled at the memory. "Yes, I liked that one. Very nice. The urinal cracked in half like an egg. Also, there was the time the five sets of twins ran across the street and tackled you."

"They were all dressed like waiters at Denny's."

"Very nice. Very nice indeed," David Lynch said loudly. "Well, I guess I'll be going. I can't keep Isabella Rossellini waiting all night."

"I'm going to meet her one of these times. I'm sure of it."

"Yes! You keep dreaming, fella."

"You don't even know my name, do you?"

"It's hard to keep track. I'm in a lot of people's dreams, you know!" He tossed me a lifelike doll of the *Eraserhead* baby. It let out its grating cry.

I set the *Eraserhead* baby down on the sidewalk. "Keep an eye on things," I told it. It wailed. I walked down the street where I used to live, before I was locked up in the VA booby hatch. Before my divorce. The street crumbled under my feet, turning into gravel and then dust. The sun zoomed up in the sky. Grass grew under my feet and off in all directions. Dandelions bloomed. Bees buzzed.

Katie the dog bounded up to me, a tennis ball in her mouth. She dropped it at my feet and barked. I threw the ball. She bounded off after it. It was a perfect day. Everything was perfect. We played like that for a while. A dog's dream! No wonder Katie preferred this. It was mindless. It was fun.

But the sun grew hotter and the dandelions wilted. The wind picked up and dust blew into my eyes. Katie the person stood next to me. "What are you doing?"

"I'm not doing anything," I said.

"You're doing this. This isn't a dog's dream. This is the other kind of dream. The kind I don't like."

"Why didn't you stay a dog?"

"You think I want to dream as a person? This is you."

We were where we had to be. We were at FOB Eagle. The sun dipped down over the horizon. We heard rhythmic clapping. We heard a chant.

"Not this," Katie said.

"Not what?"

"You don't remember."

"I don't."

"Come with me. Let's get this over with." She was in full battle rattle, minus her weapon. I was wearing an Army PT t-shirt, baggy shorts and shower shoes. She walked off ahead of me. "Come on. Let's go. You're the one who dreamed this up."

I followed her to the dee-fac. Inside, there was everyone in headquarters and headquarters company. They were pounding on the tables, facing a small stage. On the stage was Fun Boss Todd, a robust retired chief petty officer in the Navy, who was now working as a non-appropriated fund employee of the Army at FOB Eagle. He was there, as his job title implied, to make us have fun. He was brutal about it.

"I remember Fun Boss Todd," I said.

"Great. That's who you decide to remember."

"I didn't remember him until right now."

Fun Boss Todd was standing next to a karaoke machine. Lights flashed on it. He waved a microphone in the air, and then brought it down to his enormous, cement block head to intone, "Who's next!" His voice boomed through the dee-fac. The scent of chili mac was wafting through the air. Fun Boss Todd's t-shirt said in bright red letters, "FUN BOSS." "Oh, ho-ho! Look who we have here! It's my favorite little Asian girl and her sourpuss boyfriend, the combat cartoonist! If we all clap loud enough, I bet we can make these two lovebirds sing a song! What do you say? Let's give them a big INFANTRY HOO-AH!"

"HOO-AH!" the entire company boomed out. They slapped the tables louder.

I walked up and grabbed the microphone. I was reenacting a play that I'd been in a long time ago. I was merely playing my part in the play. This stranger, this actor that I'd become, shouted into the microphone, "Tanaka's not my girlfriend!"

This elicited laughter and cheers. It also got a lot of uh-oh's. "You in trouble now, CC!" someone shouted from the crowd. "You girlfriend angry at you!" "She pissed!" another G.I. shouted. Laughter rolled through the crowd.

Katie hugged herself and glared at the rowdy company, which was becoming rowdier by the second.

Fun Boss Todd grabbed the microphone from me and said, "That's not what I heard! I heard you two sneak behind the conex boxes and play hide the sausage! Ha, ha, ha!" This generated a lot of laughter and "woo!" and "ohhh!" like we were in an episode of *Maury*.

I grabbed the microphone again and shouted into it, "We talk! We're friends!" I remembered now. I thought I was defending her honor. But the whole thing was becoming more and more deranged.

Fun Boss Todd took the microphone back from me, ripping it from my hands. He was a huge man. Burly.

I looked over at Katie. She was crying. Humiliated.

"Tanaka," I said. I remembered. We called each other by our last names back then. It was all coming back to me. Every bit of it. The good stuff and the bad. All the hanging out we did. We dreamed together, both literally and figuratively. I reached over to touch her shoulder and she shrugged away from me. She ran out of the tent.

Fun Boss Todd cued up the song he thought we should sing. He tried to hand me the microphone. I looked down at the little screen and saw the lyrics: "YOU CAN'T HURRY LOVE. YOU JUST HAVE TO WAIT. LOVE DON'T COME EASY…" I took the microphone from him and chucked it down on the ground and stomped on it.

"Hey!" Fun Boss Todd said. "You can't treat government equipment like that!" He grabbed my shoulder and spun me around. He shouldn't have done that. I was seeing red, enraged at what he'd put Katie through. And enraged at myself for my part in it. I saw a future without Katie in it, and it was beyond bleak. It was unthinkable. For the first time in my life, I hauled off and slugged someone. I felt the bone in my trigger finger crack as it connected with Fun Boss Todd's massive jaw. I hit him so hard and with such violence that his head snapped backward and he dropped to the stage floor with an enormous thud.

My fellow soldiers ate it up. "Der-LETH, Der-LETH, Der-LETH!" they chanted.

Doc walked up to me and raised my broken hand over my head. "The heavyweight champion of FOB Eagle!" Doc shouted. "King Fobbit!"

"King Fobbit! King Fobbit! King Fobbit!" they chanted.

Doc examined my hand. He leaned in and said, "Come by later and I'll tape this up. You wouldn't want to miss our mission outside the wire, would you? After all, Tanaka will be out there all alone with us if you decide to stay in the rear. Who knows what could happen to her?"

Fun Boss Todd stood up and then mock backed away from me. "Don't hit me again, big guy! Whoa, nelly!" he said, mostly to the crowd, in his basso profundo voice.

I tore my hand away from Doc, who smirked at me. I ran out of the dee-fac after Katie. I lost one of my shower shoes and then the other as I ran. I tried to guess where she might be and found her not far away, in a tent that we used to store silly string. There were boxes and boxes of silly string there, sent by people back stateside when they heard a rumor that we used it to detect invisible wires that were connected to roadside bombs.

"Tanaka!" I shouted, running up to her with bare feet.

"Go away!" she yelled at me. She turned her back to me.

"I'm sorry. I'm so sorry. I didn't mean it."

She turned toward me, her goggles off. It was so rare for me to see her eyes without the goggles that I was taken aback. I gasped a bit. "What? What are staring at?"

"I… uh. I…"

"What do you want, Derleth? What do you want from me?"

"Tanaka." My voice shook. I had to say it to her. "Tanaka, I love you."

"God damn you!" she roared. "God damn you for saying that here! Now! Your timing is fucked, Derleth. It's fucked! You get me? You're fucked!"

"Tanaka. I didn't mean it."

"That you lo-o-ove me?"

"How can I make this right?"

"Stay away from me," she said venomously. "Get away from me. Get away from me right now."

"Katie," I said weakly. It was the first time I'd used her first name. "Please. Don't."

"Get away from me."

You have to remember, we were both kids at the time. I was 17. She was 19. We'd barely lived at that point.

I backed away from her. I walked around in my bare feet, around the garrison, in circles. This had all happened. It was all real. My heart was broken. I resolved that I would leave her alone. That I wouldn't even look at her. The wind blew and dust swirled around. It was a million degrees. The sky was black and full of blurry stars. I woke up.

Katie was curled up on the foot of the bed, awake. She was human and wearing Darth Maul pajamas. She sat up and gazed at me, her face sad. Mid-afternoon sunlight filtered through the shade. She got up and walked over to me. "Push over," she said. It was a double bed. Plenty of room.

"Are those Darth Maul pajamas?"

"Yes. That's your question? After that horrible dream you forced me to have?"

"I'm afraid of shoving my foot down my own throat again. Might choke to death."

"There are no good things to say after a dream like that," she said. "You sleep naked all the time now?"

"My wife. My ex-wife. She preferred it. She said that it made me more fertile. She wanted to have five kids. Three boys and two girls. We only had the one kid. She blamed me for my lack of productivity, vis a vis children. We had a lot of reproductive sex. We were constantly tracking her fertility. I had my sperm checked. They're good-to-go. I got used to not wearing any shorts to bed. Was I oversharing just now?"

"Maybe a little." She laid down next to me on top of the sheet. She rolled over onto her side. "So. Do you remember more now?"

"I remember almost everything now."

"Almost?"

"I still don't remember the... uh. Thingie."

"When you tried to catch the RPG."

"Yes. That."

"So. Did you mean it? When you said you loved me?"

"Yes. I meant it. I couldn't imagine my life without you. I can't imagine my life without you now."

"Well. Good. I'm glad we got that settled. What took you so long to say it? We spent so much time together and you never bothered to tell me that. You could have slipped that in sometime during one of our arguments about *Star Wars* versus *Star Trek*."

"When people are kind to me, especially women, I try not to read too much into it. It makes me seem timid, and maybe I am."

"You thought I was being kind to you?"

"You were being kind to me. You were giving me your friendship. What could be more kind?"

"Phil," she said. "Phil, I want you to look at me." I'd turned my head toward the window without thinking about it. I looked over at her. "Kiss me, you stupid, stupid man."

I rolled over onto my side, leaned in, and we gently touched our lips together, slowly working up to a real kiss. I held her close, and she held me. It was one of those kisses where you're transported somewhere between reality and a dream. Maybe it was the first real kiss in my life. It felt like it.

When we were done, I fell back on the bed. Katie put her head on my shoulder and I put my arm around her shoulders, and we drifted off to sleep together. In our new dream, we were surfing again, out on the Pacific Ocean, not a care in the world. She was a good teacher. Patient.

We were sitting on the beach, staring out of the waves, our toes in the sand, our hair crusty with dried saltwater, when we heard the distant rumbling. "Earthquake?" I asked Katie.

"In a dream?" Katie asked me.

"I've never been through an earthquake. Not a real one, anyway. Is this what it's like?"

"No. This is nothing like an earthquake. They don't last this long."

We were shaken awake. The sound continued. We blinked, confused, and sat up.

"What the hell?" Katie asked.

My father stood in the doorway. "Come look out the front window. You won't believe this. Or maybe you will." He toddled away.

Katie slid out of bed. She stood in the middle of the room in her Darth Maul pajamas, hands on her hips. "You'd better put on your clothes."

"Yeah, I guess I'd better." I got up out of bed, naked, and she slapped me on the ass.

DUTCH MASTERS

The three of us stared out the front window at the mess on the street. Directly in front of our driveway, there was a small army of OhDOT workers digging a foot deep trench with jackhammers in one of the few places in northeast Ohio where there wasn't a pothole.

"What are they doing?" Katie asked over the racket.

"What does it look like?" my father asked. "They're taking out their revenge. It's been a long time coming."

"Guess you're not driving the car anytime soon," I said.

"You got that right," my father said. "Big deal. This is small potatoes."

The crew occupied the entire width of the street in front of our house. No one would pass by.

We went into the kitchen to figure out what to do next.

"Can you put on something different?" my father asked Katie. "What you're wearing is distracting."

"Too sexy?" Katie asked.

"Too weird. What's that supposed to be all over those pajamas? The devil?"

"It's Darth Maul," I said.

"Darth what?"

"*Star Wars*," Katie said.

"You're not gonna start talking about comic book stuff, are you?" my father asked. "You know that drives me nuts."

She stood up. She became a dog. She barked twice. She became human again. She was wearing her pink dress. It was much cleaner now. The colors were bright. Her pink basketball shoes looked brand new. She had on socks with them. "How's this?"

"Much better," my father said. "You got a whole wardrobe somewhere?"

"I never know what I'll have on when I switch back to being human," Katie said. "No idea where the clothes come from." She sat down again. She was in my mother's chair. No one had commented on it yet. My father and I simply accepted that was where Katie should sit. She kicked my leg gently under the table.

I looked over at her and she smiled. She reached over and gently grazed the top of my hand with her fingertips. She looked up at the wall. "Did you paint that?" She stood up and pulled my painting off the wall. "This is your painting? When did you paint it?"

"When he was fourteen," my father said. "Pretty good, right?"

"I feel like I could eat the fruit in this painting."

"It's not that good," I said.

"There are too many people who'll want to run you down in this life," Katie said. "You shouldn't try to beat them to the punch." She studied the painting some more. "I want you to start drawing our dreams, just like we talked about when we were in the Army."

I looked at my hands. They weren't shaking. "I haven't drawn anything in years. I'm out of practice."

"Son, it's what you're meant to do," my father said. "Like masonry is for me."

"So it's settled," Katie said, hanging the painting back the wall. "You're going to draw something for me." She made sure that the painting was hanging correctly before she sat back down.

"Yes," I said. "Maybe I'll draw you." I took in her face. I saw all the shapes in it. I realized that was how I looked at the world. I was constantly drawing in my head. Everything was a drawing to me. I looked at her skin and her dress and calculated the light and dark. The highlights. The shadows. Her cheeks. Her lips. Her blue eye and her brown eye. I already had a plan on how to draw her. I was remembering it from a long time ago. "Maybe I'll do it in the style of the old Dutch masters." Is this really happening? I wondered. I'm I really going to do this? Am I me again? What did it mean if I was? I sat staring at Katie and she stared back at me. A loud knock on the door shook me out of my reverie. "I'll get it," I said.

I opened the front door and standing there was my old crush, Patty McGinty, with her blond hair and pale skin, her blue-green eyes like the sea. She pushed into the house past me. "What the hell is going on out in front of your house?" she shouted.

"We can hear you just fine," my father said.

"I can't even hear myself think," Patty said. "This have something to do with your stray?" She pointed over at Katie.

"Don't," I said, holding up a finger. "Don't."

"So what is this? I'm over here visiting my dad and now I can't get out of here. My nine-year-old son wants to eat at McDonald's and if I don't take him, he's gonna go ballistic. That kid is gonna be the death of me, I swear to Christ."

"Sorry about that," I said.

"And the noise! How can you just sit here like nothing's happening? Shouldn't she be howling right about now? Baying at the moon? One of you should go talk to them! Find out what you did to piss off the guild."

We already knew what we'd done to piss of the guild, but I wasn't going to say that to Patty. "I'll go talk to them," I said. "Maybe they'll listen to reason."

"That's the spirit."

"They're not going to listen to you, son," my father said. "I'm lettered. I should go out there."

"Their beef isn't with you, dad. It's with me. For helping you out."

Patty glared at each of us in turn. "I still say it has something to do with that stray you took in."

I felt the back of my neck get hot. "Get out of my house, Patty," I said, angrily. "And don't come back."

"Fine," she said. "I'll leave you weirdoes to hang out with a dog-girl." She stomped out the door and slammed it behind her.

I turned to say something to Katie, but she'd already turned back into a dog. The dog was wet and shaking, like someone had tossed a bucket of water on her. She whined and ran out of the room toward the side door, and then down into the basement.

I ran into the bathroom and grabbed a towel. I went down the steps into the basement and found her curled in a corner. I dried her off. She yipped and cried. "Don't let assholes like Patty define you," I said.

Katie phased back over to human. She had on stained and ripped jeans. Her grimy basketball shoes were falling apart. She had on a threadbare t-shirt with "Rock N Roll" written in faded neon script on the front. She was damp and shivering, like she'd been caught out in the rain. "Look at me. I'm a mess," she said.

"We both need work," I said. "We should both have warning signs posted. Flashing yellow lights."

"Caution tape," she said. "A guy with a sign that says, 'Slow' on one side and 'Stop' on the other."

"It all follows us around. A big parade."

The house shook, like there had been an explosion.

"That Chestnut guy is a creep," Katie said, her hands over her ears.

"I'd better go out front and see what's going on."

"Be careful."

"I will."

I climbed the stairs and went directly out the side door. I strode down the driveway and walked over to the man holding a clipboard in a the cleanest OhDOT uniform. He was standing in the middle of what used to be our street. It was now a large foot-deep gravel pit, with all of the asphalt stripped away.

"Okay, pal. We get it. No need for the explosions," I said.

"Sir, I have a work order right here."

"Work order."

"Signed by Deputy Undersecretary of Transportation Merle Chestnut. You can see his signature at the bottom, authorizing this emergency road closure."

"Imagine that," I said.

"We have full authority to take whatever measures are necessary to ensure that this stretch of road…"

"Directly in front of our driveway."

"…is fully attenuated. The roadway had an overly thick surface which could have led to a buckling situation."

"I see."

"It's all right here in the work order, sir. Paragraph seven-bee. As you can see, I am following the orders of Deputy Undersecretary of Transportation Merle Chestnut. He is the deciding authority in situations requiring road attenuation."

"Uh-huh."

"Oh, and sir?"

"Yes."

"Watch yourself." The man took two steps back.

"Watch myself?" I asked, right before a tan Plymouth hit me going about twenty miles per hour. I tumbled over the hood of the car, rolled over the roof, thumped onto the trunk, and flopped back first onto the gravelized road. The car slid to a halt about twenty meters away from me. I saw all the little pockmarks of rust. It was Patty's car. I thought, "Boy, she didn't take getting tossed out of the house well at all." I coughed up a bit of blood.

The door opened, and a tow-headed boy stepped out of it. He ran over and crouched next to me. "I didn't see you!" he shouted in my face. It was less a declaration than an accusation. Like maybe I shouldn't be standing in the torn-up street in case a child decides to steal his mother's car for a McDonald's run. "You dented the car. My mom's gonna be pissed!"

I'd bitten my tongue. That's where the blood was coming from. I was a little dizzy. I think I'd hit my head somewhere along the way. My breathing hurt like hell. I was pretty sure I'd broken at least a few ribs. I sat up and then fell back down.

Katie arrived a moment later, still dressed in her street kid clothes.

"Katie, go back inside," I said.

"I'm hungry," Patty's son said. He tromped back to his stolen vehicle, got back in, and peeled out, throwing gravel all over the place.

"That kid has a bright future ahead of him," I said.

Katie laughed. Then she peered in at my face. "There's blood."

"I bit my tongue. Help me up," I said.

"No. You should stay down."

"That's the stray," I heard one of the workers say.

"Confirmed. That's the stray."

Katie turned into a dog and growled at them, baring her teeth. They backed off. Way off.

"This isn't worth a hundred bucks."

"Merle's cheap."

She became human again, again in her street clothes. We heard an ambulance siren coming down the road. We listened to it get closer.

"You should go inside," I told Katie. "It's going to be all right. I'll be fine. They'll patch me up and I'll come home right away."

"No," Katie said. "Last time they wouldn't let me go with you. Then they wouldn't tell me where you'd gone."

"It's not like last time. This is Cleveland, not Iraq. I think I only have a few cracked ribs. Maybe a deep bruise on my thigh."

"I'm not leaving you." She turned her head skyward and let out a mournful howl. She was still human.

The ambulance pulled up. A pair of paramedics walked over. One of them leaned down and smiled at me. It was a familiar face, but not a welcome one.

"Hello, Doc," I said. "Hello, John Wayne."

"Oh, fuckity fuck. What do we have here? Is this CC? Could it be you? The saddest-ass soldier it was ever my displeasure to tend to. You catch another RPG there, CC?"

"He got run over by a car, you jackass," Katie said.

"Holy shit! It's Tanaka! Fuck, man. And she's a stray! That's fucking hilarious. What's your deal, troop? You put out a little kibble for your girlfriend every night just before you fuck her?"

I tried to get to my feet, but John Wayne pushed me back down. "Don't move. We don't need you rupturing a spleen or anything." John Wayne Bostick, by the look of him, had been working out. His arms were bulging. His thighs were the size of pony kegs.

His size didn't seem to bother Katie, who leapt at him, knocking him backward onto the hood of his ambulance. She grabbed him by the front of his shirt and slammed him repeatedly on the hood. "Fix him!" Katie shouted. "You didn't fix him last time, and he was broken! You better fix him, or I'll hurt you. I'll rip your fucking throat out!"

Doc seemed a bit afraid and a bit amused. "I don't fix people. I keep them alive. Other people fix people. That's their job, not mine. Ask me, he was broken before the Army. Broke dick soldier." We heard another set of sirens coming. "That'll be the cops. You want them to catch you out in the open, Tanaka? You know what they do to strays in this town when they catch them?" He leered at her. "Tell you what. You're so concerned about ol' CC here, why don't you ride along? I'm sure he could use the company. Fuck. We'll catch up. Talk about the good old days in Iraq. Those hajis you zapped with the fifty-cal, for instance. Man, you sure killed the shit out of them."

She let go of him. He walked around the back of the ambulance along with the other paramedic. She went with them and disappeared into the ambulance. They returned with the gurney. They slipped a board underneath me and strapped me tightly to it and then put me on the gurney. Soon enough, I was loaded into the ambulance. The doors swung shut. Katie sat looking at me, worried.

Doc started an IV, put a bag of saline up, and then shot some morphine into the line. I immediately felt the morphine take hold. It was a familiar sensation, even all these years later. I was pumped full of morphine for almost a month after I was wounded. That sort of drugging changes you. It changes your brain. I was different on morphine. I cared about nothing. I liked the feeling.

Katie took my hand and got closer to me.

"I gotta call this one in," Doc John Wayne said. He picked up a handheld radio and checked in with dispatch. Then he said, "I got a code eight-six-seven-five-three-oh-nine, over."

"Eight-six-seven-five-three-oh-nine, copy," the dispatcher said.

"What does that mean?" I asked.

"Oh, it's just a code. Like a FRAGO. Don't mean nothing." He pulled out a syringe. "Here, have a second order of fries." He sent more morphine into my bloodstream. Now I was loopy.

"Oh my God," Katie went. "He doesn't look good."

"He's fine. He's on my bus. People on my bus don't die. Strictly forbidden. Ain't that right, brother?" He shouted to the driver.

"Fuck yeah!" the driver shouted back.

"See. It's all good."

"Almost there. Brace for impact," the driver shouted back to us.

"You see any ACO's out there?"

"Whuz an ay-cee-oh?" I slurred out.

"You'll find out in a second, big man. Combat. Cartoonist. Big man. Shit, dude. You got some scary-ass scars on your head. I feel kind of honored that I was there to see them made."

"What's an 'ACO'?" Katie asked.

"About a hundred bucks for me," Doc said. "Fifty, if me and my bud up front split it. I'm feeling generous, frankly."

The ambulance came to a stop. The doors popped open and two men dressed in all white uniforms stood there. One of them held a long pole with a loop of wire at one end. The other held a long pole with a buzzing green light at the end of it.

"Nice doggy," the man with the loop said.

Katie's eyes widened. She tried to scramble away, but there was nowhere to hide. The man with the loop was quick. He slipped the loop around Katie's neck and pulled her toward the back of the ambulance. She grabbed at the loop and the pole, but she was no match for the large man. He easily tugged her toward him.

"No! You don' unnerstan," I heard myself slurring. "She's no stray. She's muh-muh girl an I luv her…" I struggled, but Doc had strapped me down tightly and shot me so full of morphine that I couldn't keep a thought, much less move. "Katie!" I shouted "Katie!"

The second animal control officer prodded Katie with his stick. She glowed green for a moment, and then she was a dog again. She was skinny and missing fur. She yowled. A second prodding with the green glow stick made her pass out. They shoved her in a tiny cage and tossed the cage up into a truck that was stacked with cages. Every cage had a dog in it.

"Katie!" I shouted, straining at my straps.

"Katie!" Doc shouted, mocking me. "Boo-fucking-hoo. I never liked that chick. You know, she never put out for anyone but you at Camp Chickenshit. That seemed undemocratic given the lack of tail in those environs. Anyway, time to sleep." He laid another shot into my IV line and blackness swamped me, sucking me downward into a deep, bottomless pit.

ENTER THE CHIHUAHUA

I awoke to the screams of my fellow patients. I opened my eyes and an interested fellow stood at the foot of my bed. He was reading something off of a clipboard. The drop ceiling above my head had a spreading yellow stain in it. The lights were florescent and blinding. I could smell a whiff of ammonia in the air. The interested fellow asked me how I was feeling.

"I can't tell," I said. I felt numb and dizzy.

He handed me a clear contraption with a place for me to blow into. Inside the contraption was a tiny green ball. "Blow in here," he said, pointing at the hose and mouthpiece, "and make the ball float. It'll keep your lungs from collapsing."

"Who are you?" I asked.

"I'm your doctor," he said. He wore blue scrubs and a white lab coat. He reached into the pocket of the lab coat and produced a syringe. "This should help."

I fell asleep. I never saw him again.

I awoke to the screams of my fellow patients. I opened my eyes and an interested lady stood at the foot of my bed. She was reading something off of a clipboard. The stain in the drop ceiling had spread out to the size of a garbage can lid. The lights were brighter now. Whiter. The scent of ammonia in the air had been replaced with the scent of pine trees. The interested lady asked me how I was feeling.

"I can't tell," I said. I felt numb and dizzy.

She pulled out a little light and checked my eyeballs and my tongue.

"Who are you?" I asked.

"I'm your doctor," she said. She wore blue scrubs and a white lab coat. She reached into the pocket of the lab coat and produced a syringe. "Let's adjust your meds by just a smidge."

I fell asleep. I never saw her again.

I awoke to the screams of my fellow patients. I opened my eyes and an interested person stood at the foot of my bed. He or she was reading something off of a clipboard. The stain in the drop ceiling was shaped like a massive spider web. A viscous yellow blob hung precariously from a spot just above the person's head. The interested person said something. I wasn't sure what it was. I kept my mouth shut. The interested person slipped a blood pressure cuff around my upper arm. More words came out. Indistinct.

The person came into focus. For a moment, I thought it was Ohio Deputy Undersecretary of Transportation Merle Chestnut, but I was mistaken. It was a woman, a different woman this time. Blue scrubs, white lab coat. She said, "Does anybody really know what time it is? Does anybody really care?"

Three orderlies popped their heads inside my room and sang in harmony, "Care what time!" and disappeared.

"Who are you?" I asked.

"I'm your doctor," she said.

"I need… I need to get out of here," I said. "I need to go." I realized that my arms and legs were tied down with thick, padded restraints. "Where am I?"

"You're in a charity hospital," the doctor said. "You're being cared for by a consortium of charitable foundations, many of whom also sponsor your favorite programs on PBS. Remember *Sandusky Memories*? That was a good show, right?"

I struggled. I realized that I had nothing on but a hospital gown. "Where are my clothes?"

"You need to rest. To get better. Have you been blowing into this?" She held up the device my original doctor had brought in.

"I'm always asleep. What day is this?"

"That's not a good sign, not knowing what day it is. Have you experienced a bowel movement lately?"

"I'm strapped to a bed."

"I know that. I'm your doctor. I know that."

"They took my girlfriend away. They put her in a cage."

"I see from your chart that you're an Iraq war veteran. Have you tried Amphion B? Amphion B gives you a heightened lack of awareness of your situation in life. Ask your doctor today about Amphion B!"

"Didn't you just tell me that you're my doctor?"

"It's all so confusing being in a hospital, isn't it Mister Derleth? This should help," she said, and she produced another syringe.

I fell asleep. I never saw her again.

I awoke. My ribs and my leg. Pain. The pain was intense. "Bone pain is the worst pain," I said aloud. "Mom," I said. "I'm sorry, Mom. I'm so sorry. I'm sorry I didn't come home. I'm sorry I'm such a shitty son. I love you! I'm sorry." I wept horribly. I wept for her, my mother, imagining the pain she'd endured and the pain I put her through.

A nurse walked by and said, "Here. Let me help you." She pushed a button on a wired remote control next to my hand. I heard a soft beep. I drifted back into sleep.

I awoke. My father was asleep in a wooden rocking chair next to my bed. I'd been rolled into another room, I realized. There were three others in there with me. All three of them were screaming, but not in unison. Sometimes they paused to gasp for air.

A woman in pink scrubs walked in. "How are we today, Mister Park?" she asked the first man.

He stared at her and let loose an open-mouthed scream.

"I'll be back later to check on your vitals."

I looked around and realized that all of us were strapped down to our rolling beds.

"Dad!" I went. "Psst! Dad!" How the hell could he sleep through all this racket?

The nurse went to the next man in the room. "How are we today, Mister Abumwe?"

He said, his voice shaking, "Bats! Bats!"

"I'll be back in a few minutes to check on your vitals."

He resumed screaming about bats.

She came to me next. "How are we today, Mister Derleth?"

"Hi," I said, trying to be as inoffensive as possible. "I'm fine."

"I'm so glad to hear that," she said. "You look like you're ready to be moved to a different ward."

"Is that good?"

"Oh, yes. That's very good." She leaned in confidentially. "I mean, take a look around." She spun her index finger near her temple, rolled her eyes and stuck out her tongue.

"There's a lot of screaming in here."

"Tell me about it." She checked my blood pressure, listened to my heart, looked into my eyes and mouth with a tiny flashlight. "If I untie you, you aren't going to run amok, are you?"

"Scout's honor," I said.

"He was never a scout," my father said. He stood up slowly. "Oh, my aching back," he said with a groan. He buzzed for a moment, flipped like a playing card over to Ronald Reagan in a TV western, and then popped back.

The nurse said, "Metaphysical Adjustment Disorder. We're seeing a lot of it these days. You should see a philosopher about that."

"We have a guy coming up from Columbus next week," I said.

"That's this week, son," my father said. "You've been in here for a while."

"Where's Katie?" I asked him.

"I don't know," he said. "Chestnut knows, but I haven't been able to find him. He hasn't been to the guild hall lately. I have some leads that I'm checking out."

"How much longer do I have to stay here?" I asked the nurse.

"You're under observation," she said. "Until you stabilize. You keep shouting, 'Katie! Katie!' It's a little weird because there's no one here with that name. Your doctor subscribed you Amphion B. Just like my flashlight." She showed me her little flashlight. It was a drug company giveaway with the Amphion B motto stamped on it: *For a heightened lack of awareness of your situation in life.*

"I do feel less aware," I said.

"That's terrific. We've found that the more aware people are, the more they scream. Like these guys. Let's have you rolled into another ward. And then we can take your restraints off."

"Thanks," I said.

"All you have to do, if you feel any pain, is push this little button right by your left hand. You can only press it ten times an hour before it stops working."

"I'm good," I said. "What's in it?"

"Morphine mixed with Amphion B. They go together like waffles and syrup," the nurse said, slapping her hands together.

"You took quite a beating from the car that ran you over." She reached over the top of me and pushed the button. I instantly felt floaty. "That's better, right?"

"I… need… to get up…" I fell asleep.

I awoke in another ward. It was night. I was in a semi-private room. The patient next to me was surrounded by curtains. He yodeled a bit and paused, like he was waiting for an echo.

I heard the click of nails on flooring and looked down. A chihuahua was on the floor, staring up at me with wet, bulgy eyes.

"How'd you get in here?" I asked him.

He clicked over to being human. "I am El Chicharrón," he said. "I go where I please." He was dressed as a hospital orderly. He was a short man with a neatly trimmed Van Dyke, his thick, black hair slicked back with pomade. He pulled the IV out of my arm. "They got you on a drip of that Amphion B shit," he said. "They always do that when they grab you."

"Where's Katie?" I asked him.

"We were hoping you'd know," El Chicharrón said. "I was the one who made Katie. Made her into a proud Siberian Husky. It's a lifestyle choice."

"So I've heard," I said.

El Chicharrón unstrapped me. "You took her in. Mad respect for anyone who takes in a stray in this town. I figured out who you were after I saw you at Ziska's Tavern. You're that dude she served with. In Iraq. She talked about you. She told me that you two dreamed together when you were over there. It was your dreams that brought her to Cleveland. She couldn't go home. Couldn't face it, for some reason. She wouldn't tell me why. She said you two talked over there. Kept each other sane."

"That's right," I said.

"Marine Corps." He thumped himself on the chest. "Served in Kandahar. Came home and looked around and thought, what the fuck is the matter with this world? DeAndre, the older gentleman you saw? He brought me into the pack. He was a soldier, like you. Vietnam. I found Katie sleeping on a bus stop bench, and brought her into the pack. No one fucks with homeless veterans on my street. That's the law of the pack." He finished untying me. He stripped off his uniform and stood there in his skivvies. "They gonna keep you in here until someone puts down Katie. You gotta find her. Get her out. ACO's got stashes of strays all over the city. In secret kennels. Takes 'em a while to get around to putting us down. So many of us locked up. I've escaped four times myself. Put this shit on. They won't even look twice at you."

"What'll you wear?"

"I don't need nothing," El Chicharrón said. "Follow me." He clicked over to being a chihuahua.

I put on the uniform. It was ridiculously undersized for me. My ribs hurt. I'd developed a limp. I had no shoes on, only hospital socks with rubber tread on the bottom. I followed him out of the room and into an antiseptic corridor. The lights buzzed overhead. A patient stood outside his room, smoking a cigarette, his hair all over the place. He winked at me and blew a smoke ring up to the ceiling. El Chicharrón sped up and so did I. We went through one set of swinging doors and then another. We rushed into an open elevator. I pushed the button labeled "L" and the doors shut. We went down with a whoosh.

The elevator doors opened. A security guard stood there. He was chatting with John Wayne Bostick.

"Where is she?" I shouted at him.

Doc turned slowly around. "Well. Look who's up."

"I asked you a question, Bostick. You fucking piece of shit. Tell me where she is."

"Tanaka's gone, troop. She's in the system. The system ain't gonna give her back to you. The system's built for winners, not for losers. America!"

El Chicharrón had scooted out of sight.

The security guard drew his pistol.

"Put that away," Doc told him. "You don't need that. This guy's a pussy. You know what he did in the service? He drew fucking pictures."

"You can do that?" the guard asked. "How the fuck you get a skate job like that?"

"Fuck if I know," Doc said. "Ask him."

"I will snap you in two, you piece of shit," I said, rage boiling inside me. "Tell me where she is."

"Make me."

"Okay," said El Chicharrón from behind him. "We'll make you." Standing around him were a whole pack of strays, some of them human and some of them big dogs.

"You don't scare me," Doc said, turning around. "Bunch of strays. You're nobody. Disposable. Like tissue paper. I'll fetch a bucket of water and watch you run."

The security guard reached for his gun.

"No, buddy," El Chicharrón said. "You put that gun away. Go out front and smoke a cigarette. Think about your life. Your choices."

The security guard did what he was told. We were alone with John Wayne Bostick.

"Bunch of pussies. What're you waiting for?" Doc asked. "Come and get it."

Before the pack could do anything, I limped over, rared back and slugged him right on the chin. This time, I bruised my ring finger.

Doc tumbled to the ground and into a swarm of dogs and people who set upon him, biting and gouging. This went on for maybe ten, fifteen seconds before El Chicharrón called out, "Stop!"

Bostick sat up, jazzed on all the violence. "Do your worst, pooches. I got nothing for you. They didn't tell me where they were taking her. Wait." He pulled his wallet out of his back pocket and took out two twenties and a ten. He slapped the money on the shiny terrazzo floor. "That's the fifty bucks I made turning her in." He laughed and shook his head. "She should have fucked me when we were in Iraq. I asked real nice."

"Did you...?"

"Did I what? Rape her? Thought about it, but no. All that battle rattle she had on? Too much work for not enough—"

I felt his nose break when I slugged him the second time. His head hit the floor with a sickening thump.

DeAndre checked his pulse. "He's alive. People like him? They don't die. Good people die all the time. Don't worry about this one. He belongs to the pack. Pack justice." He pointed at the door. "Get out of here. You got a car waiting."

I shook the hurt out of my hand. "I've gotta stop punching people," I said, like I'd somehow made a habit of it. I limped out the door, past the security guard, who was smoking, and out to a cherry mid-nineteen-sixties Mustang with my father behind the wheel. I slid into the front seat beside him.

"Son, what happened to you over there... Iraq. I'm sorry about that. I'm sorry about what happened to Katie, too. I promise I'll help you find her."

"Don't get sentimental on me now, old man. It's too late in the day for that. I need you to be the hardass you've always been."

"Jesus H. Christ, son. I'm no hardass. I'm just a jerk."

"Then be a jerk, dad. Let's hit the road."

"Grab the map out of the glove compartment, dummy. We've got work to do." I opened up the glove compartment and found a map of metro Cleveland. There were circles in black and red X's over the top of about half of them. "Those are all the old dog pounds that I could find through my contacts. If you need a change of clothes, I brought some. They're in the back seat."

I climbed over the top of the seat and changed in the back while my father drove to the closest dog pound on the map that he hadn't X'd off yet. I realized I had on my jeans from my first night of work. I pulled the key out of the pocket, the one that was supposed to open up a prize.

We drove up to the first dog pound, which was located in a night darkened alley. We could hear desperate barking coming from inside. I limped over to the door, which was made of heavy iron. I slipped the key into the lock and it clunked open.

"Where'd you get that key?" my father asked.

"It was a gift," I said. "From that mindfulness guru. That Zinn Prak Dopp guy."

"He was on your mother's stories," my father said. "He seemed like a phony to me."

"The phoniness was an act. I think he tried to tell me that when I took him to the airport. I think he wanted to tell me about this key." I slipped the key back into my pocket and pushed the door open wide. There was no attendant on duty. I pulled a switch and klieg lights glowed to life. Dozens of dogs were crammed into tiny, filthy cages. They had dry water dishes and empty bowls.

"This is a nightmare," my father muttered. "What kind of…" He whistled. "Jesus H. Christ." He walked around the dog pound in a shuffle, opening each dog's cage door.

Dogs hopped out, stumbled around a bit, and became indigent men and women, all in various states of shabby dress. They coughed and spat on the ground. They patted me and my father on the back. "Thanks, brother," they said to my father.

"Thanks, brother," they said to me.

"Do you know Katie?" we asked them.

"Don't know no Katie," they said.

"Never heard of no Katie," they said.

"Katie who?" they said.

When the last of them was freed and they stumbled out into the night, one woman came back to me. She was in her late forties, maybe. Or maybe life had aged her cruelly. Silver hair whirled around her head. She wore a field jacket with the division patch of the 101st Airborne on her upper right sleeve. "I ain't seen Katie for a while, but I heard she got caught. She was always good to me. She shared with me when she had a good situation."

"Where will you go?"

"Me? I was caught last night. I'll find somewhere to sleep. Under a house maybe. Those ACO's, they don't say nothing when they catch you. Just put that noose around your neck and zap you with the stinger. Then you're stuck as a dog until someone helps you out. Anyway, that's how it feels. Dogs need people. That's a fact. But some people, they ain't got no use for dogs. Or people. That's a fact, too."

"You should run," I said, clicking off the lights and closing the door of the dog pound. "Get away while you can."

"Your kindness made me human again," the lady said. "But I can't run as a human, only as a dog." She clicked over to being a dog. The dog wasn't in much better shape than the lady. Her muzzle was white and her eyes were cloudy. She looked up at me with her cloudy eyes, barked once, and ran off into the alley.

My father and I went to five more dog pounds, and found much the same situation in each of them. But we didn't find Katie, and no one else fessed up to knowing her.

We had the radio on in the car early in the evening. The Cavs fought the Golden State Warriors to a game seven that would be played in the Gund. My father had tickets. Cleveland would lose. We always lose, no matter how close we come to victory. We had no thought of going. We only thought of freeing Katie, wherever she was. Priorities.

The sun came up over Cleveland. It didn't look nearly as pretty as it had on the day I shared Sheila's ice cream with Katie. Nothing looked good. My father and I went home and each collapsed on our respective bed.

I woke up in pain. My ribs hurt. My leg throbbed. I looked over at my Big Ben alarm clock. It had stopped ticking. I'd forgotten to wind it. I was fully clothed. I'd been so tired when we got home that I hadn't even bothered to disrobe.

I pulled the key out of my pocket. I gripped it tightly in my fist, hoping that somehow it connected me to Katie. I never really learned to casually like someone. Even with my wife, I was consumed with her, even after I began to realize I didn't even like her that much. We didn't have anything in common. She was preoccupied with money—both spending it and hoarding it. Still, I obsessed on her wants and needs. She once asked me, while we were driving to a movie, what it would take to make me happy. She pointed out that I always seemed pensive, and not in a good way. "I want you to be happy. That would make me happy," I said. Just a smile out of her every once in a while would have meant the world to me. But I didn't know how to make her happy, and that was frustrating. We were two very different people. Our daughter was just like her. "Loser Dad," I muttered aloud, winding my alarm clock. "What time is it?" I asked aloud. I looked around for my phone and couldn't find it. I dug through my memory and realized that Katie had it. I ran to the kitchen to dial my own number.

The phone rang four times, and then I heard my voice. "This is Phil Derleth of Caldwell and Beech. Please leave a name and a contact number or email address so I can further serve your needs. Thank you for being a client."

I called two more times and got my voicemail twice more. She must not have turned the phone back on. Maybe she didn't even realize she had it. Or it was in the other dimension where her human body was trapped, while her dog body was crammed in a tiny cage, sick and awaiting a needle. My heart raced and I hyperventilated. I blacked out.

I awoke to my mother's ghost kneeling over me. "And he's back," she said.

I sat up on the kitchen floor. I smelled waffles, real waffles, in the waffle iron. There was a whole stack of them on a plate. "Mom. What are you doing?"

"Ghosts are just a set of habits, sweetheart," my mother said. "My habit was cooking for you."

"You didn't have me until you were thirty-six," I said. "You had other habits."

"I worked," my mother said. "I scrubbed floors for a family in Shaker Heights. I worked the china counter at Halle's department store downtown. I rubbed your father's back when he came home. He wasn't always a jerk. He wasn't a bad man. He owned a convertible AMC Rebel before the AMC Rambler. The Rebel was maroon. I may have fallen in love with the car as much as the man. It was a beauty."

I got up off the floor and limped over to my chair. "The Rebel," I said. "I remember hearing about that car."

"Yes. You're remembering things now. Your life. I didn't like that woman you married. There was something wrong with her. No, not so much with her. With the two of you together. You're a dreamer, you know. You got that from me. I got it from my father, who got it from his father. That girl you're looking for? She's a dreamer, too. You have to find her."

"I will, Mom."

"You're only a Derleth in name. You're a Healy, through and through. Remember that."

"He's stuck with my name, Marie," my father said, staggering into the kitchen with his sore back. He sat down in his chair and groaned. "But listen to your mother, son. You're a dreamer. Don't stop being one. And draw something when this whole thing's over, for fuck's sake. Make something out of the dreams you have with that girl. Jesus H. Christ."

"Larry, what have I told you about blasphemy in my kitchen?"

"It's strictly forbidden. I'll wash my mouth out with soap later."

"Come get your waffles," my mother said. "I'd bring them over, but I get less substantial the further I get away from this sink. Or rather, what's under this sink."

"What's under the sink?" my father asked, puzzled.

"Nothing," I said.

"Then what's the big deal?"

"When I say 'nothing,' I mean absolutely nothing. It's black. There's nothing under there. Not even Bon Ami," I said, getting up to limp over and pick up the two plates. I placed them on the table and went back to get margarine and syrup. My mother had made coffee, so I poured us each a cup. "I'd pour you a cup, Mom, but…"

"Yeah, yeah," she went. "It would go right through me." She held out her hands, palms up. "C'mon. That's a joke. Lighten up, you two."

"Got it," my father said. "Come sit with us. You can sit over here, can't you?"

My mother walked over and sat down on her chair. She was transparent. "My boys. Look at you two, sitting together. I thought I'd never see it again."

"Marie, how's the afterlife? Is there room for one more?" my father asked.

"You haven't touched your food, Larry. I'm a little insulted."

My father buttered his waffles and poured syrup on them. He cut them into little squares and ate a few. "Excellent, as always."

"What about you, Phil? Aren't you going to eat? You'll waste away to nothing."

"I'm worried about Katie," I said.

"You'll find her tonight," my mother said. "You and your father. You have to go to the game."

"To the finals?" my father asked.

"You still have the tickets, don't you?" my mother asked.

My father slapped his ass twice, the side with the wallet. "Right here."

"That's how you'll find her."

"How?" I asked.

"You'll figure that out," my mother said with a sly grin. She touched the side of her nose with her index finger and faded away.

My father slapped his fork on the table and shouted up at the ceiling, "Very dramatic, Marie!"

She faded back in for a moment and said, "Thanks, Larry," and faded away again.

We finished eating. My father was cleaning up when we heard a rap on the side door. I limped over and opened it, and my uncle pushed right past me into the house. He was drunk as a preacher on a Sunday morning and it wasn't even dark yet.

"Where's my sister?" he asked.

"In the ground," my father said. "You'd know that if you'd bothered to show up for the funeral."

"I was at sea," my uncle said. "Or I was drunk. Let's go with 'drunk.'" He sat down on my mother's chair. "Marie! Marie, you sweet darling! Come on out! Peek-a-boo!"

"How'd you hear about the ghost?" I asked him.

"Some chatty OhDOT fucker I ran into at Ziska's Tavern told me all about it. Said when he was bricking up the street out front, he saw a ghostly woman through the front window trying to turn on the TV. I said, 'That was my sister, you bastard!' I came right over."

"You have some things you need to say? I can pass them on," I said.

"Thanks for the offer, my nutty nephew, but I don't think I can trust you to remember jack shit, considering the condition of your noggin."

"Then I'll pass it on," my father said.

"It's of a personal nature."

"You're wondering where Marie put all of her savings bonds," my father said.

"That may end up being a point of discussion," my uncle said.

"Even though she left all of her worldly possessions to me."

"She owed me a bit of money, let's say. From when we were younger. From when this one was born," he said, thumping my upper arm. "From when she had to quit her jobs washing rich men's floors and selling china to their wives."

"I spent the bonds. Cashed them in and spent them. Spent every dime," my father said. "You need liquor money, you've come to the wrong place."

"Heard my nephew here picked up a stray," my uncle said. "Some people might pay good money for news about a stray."

"You're too late for that one, too," my father said. "Someone already turned her in. She's gone."

"Get out of my house," I said.

"Look, I know you think I killed your dog, but it isn't true. Omar was suicidal. Probably came from being with a sour-faced boy who could never enjoy himself."

"Get out," I said. "Get out now."

"Marie's only son, and he's just as sour as she was. And judgmental, too."

"Get out before I throw you out."

"You? You think you could… hey!" I grabbed him by the shirt collar and dragged him to the front door. "This is no way to treat family!"

"Goodbye, Liam!" my father shouted gaily. "Come back anytime!"

I swung open the door and tossed him down the front steps. I slammed the door shut. "So we're going to the game tonight?"

"Looks that way." My father finished the washing-up. He opened the cabinet doors under the sink. He crouched down and peered inside. "You weren't kidding. Whole lot of nothing down here. I think I hear something." He leaned in and I pulled him back from the brink by his shoulders.

"You don't want to do that. You could fall in. There might not be a bottom."

"There's a bottom. There's always a bottom."

I helped my father to his feet. "Dad, why are you helping me? You never took an interest before."

"You smile when she's around."

"That's it?"

"Yeah, that's it. You're a better man with her. I want you to be a better man."

"Let's get ready to go. We'll go to the muni lot first. Look around."

We each retired to our own shower. After my shower, I got it in my head that I needed to clean the tub for Katie. That she would need some quality time after her ordeal. I scrubbed the tub, the floors, the toilet. I found new towels for her. I went into the kitchen and found some emergency candles in the junk drawer. I grabbed some tea saucers and brought them in the bathroom. I'd figure out the rest later.

I put on my clothes. I didn't have anything sports-related in my closet, so I put on a plain black pocket t-shirt and my jeans. I laced a pair of old tennis shoes on. I stood up straight. I breathed in and out.

My father had on an old Craig Ehlo jersey and a baggy pair of shorts. We were an odd couple. "Taking the rapid's, or driving?" I asked him.

"Driving. We'll park in the muni."

The drive downtown was uneventful. I stared out the window, watching Cleveland go by. I'd be able to tell people that I was at another game where a Cleveland team choked when victory was at hand, I told myself. Mainly, I thought about Katie. I closed my eyes and tried to reach out to her. There was nothing there, just static.

My father turned on the radio and twirled the dial until sports talk radio came up. A couple of dudes named Dan and Dan gabbed about how the Cavs were destined to lose. Then there was a commercial for a place downtown called, "Nothing But Corn." "We got corn dogs, corn syrup, corn flakes, corn by the ear, corn by the bushel barrel. You want corn? We got corn. And it's all Ohio corn, folks. That's right. One-hundred percent Ohio corn. None of that Indiana corn. Certainly no Michigan corn. Who ever heard of such a thing? Michigan corn? Not us! Come on down and see what fifty yards of corn looks like. You know you want to. Come before the game, or after. It doesn't matter. Corn is here. Corn is tremendous. Corn! Corn! Corn!"

The muni lot was nearly full when we arrived. My father paid the fee and we drove in. Some people looked like they'd already been to Nothing But Corn. A man and his child stood near our spot, each eating an ear of corn right off the cob. Butter ran down their forearms and dripped off their elbows. Columns of smoke rose from hundreds of grills. A banner strung from one RV to another read, "CLEVELAND AGAINST THE WORLD." A man dressed like Brownie the Elf walked from one parking spot to another handing out cans of Carling Black Label. Another man dressed as Brutus Buckeye shot t-shirts out of a pneumatic cannon. Two men dressed in suits of armor had a clanging sword fight. A pair of jugglers tossed chainsaws, axes and tomato plants in old coffee cans to each other in high arcs. We watched a touch football game for a moment. "This is it!" a naked man painted head-to-toe in blue and red shouted. "It's gonna happen tonight! We're gonna win!"

We continued on to The Gund, which was next door to The Jake. The Jake had a boisterous sell-out crowd inside. They sang in unison: "We're not gonna take it! No, we ain't gonna take it! We're not gonna take it… anymore!" Someone was unlucky enough to be playing the Indians that night against a jacked-up Cleveland crowd.

We made it inside the arena and followed the arrows to our section. We climbed higher and higher. We eventually had to climb up a narrow ladder and then up a knotted rope to a section where the seats were the size of a grade-schooler's desk chair. We squished in to the middle of a row near the top of the stadium. We each wiped a drip of blood from our nostrils. Eventually, a vendor dressed top to bottom in neon green came by and sold us each a plastic cup of beer for fourteen dollars apiece. The cup already celebrated our second place finish. Even the vendors were anticipating defeat.

I kept a watchful eye around the crowd. I was looking for something, anything, that would give me a clue to where Katie was being held by the ACO's or the guild. Or OhDOT.

The game was going horribly for the Cavs, as expected. Some of the people in our section got up in disgust and left. We stuck it out.

We took turns going to the bathroom. One of us kept an eye on the game at all times. The Cavs were down by twenty at halftime. When they came back out, something miraculous happened.

The lights in the arena dimmed.

LeBron stopped halfway across the court. He looked up. The stadium camera operators noticed and showed LeBron on one jumbotron screen. On the other, was the person he was looking at.

The man stood up. He glowed.

"It's Jim Brown!" my father said, pointing. "Jim Brown!" It was indeed the great Jim Brown, who every Clevelander knows is the greatest athlete in human history. He ran for approximately ten million miles in his career as a Cleveland Brown, until Art Modell, the man who tricked Paul Brown into selling him the Browns, told Jim Brown to stop playing and leave town, thus dooming Cleveland to endless losses and heartbreak.

Art Modell later spirited the Browns out of town and made them put on humiliating purple bird uniforms. They were replaced by another team called "the Browns," but it wasn't the same. It took a while to warm to them.

Jim Brown himself had come back. He was standing. He was glowing. He pointed down to LeBron. LeBron looked up. He knelt and bowed his head. Now LeBron was glowing.

"The torch!" my father shouted. "The torch has been passed. At long last, the torch has been passed!"

From then on, through the rest of the game, LeBron was unstoppable. His vast Akron heart was three times bigger and mightier than it had been before the game. He scored sixty points in the second half, all by himself. The rest of the team sat down and watched near the end, as awestruck as the rest of us. LeBron was a god, blessed by THE god.

The game ended and my father collapsed in his seat, awash in tears. He wasn't alone. Many men in their fifties and sixties were doing the same in the crowd, overwhelmed by the victory that was unthinkable only a few short hours before.

We climbed down the knotted rope and down the ladder.

My father still hadn't composed himself. He was ashamed of his tears, of his emotion. It was un-Midwestern. I took him into the men's washroom and we ran directly into Ohio Deputy Undersecretary of Transportation Merle Chestnut, who was drying his hands under a weak blower. He was apparently unaccompanied by any of his goons.

My father, inspired by the great victory that he'd just witnessed, grabbed his old enemy by the throat and balls and slammed him into the tiled wall. "Where is she, you bastard? Where is she?"

Chestnut squealed and gagged. He couldn't speak for a variety of reasons.

"Let him down, dad. He can't talk."

My father set him down. "Say something."

"Talk," I said.

Chestnut laughed. "It's too late. You're too late." He checked his Rolex. "She was put down an hour ago at the Euclid Avenue dog pound." He laughed again. "Hey, how about that LeBron? That was pretty…" But he didn't get to finish. My father punched him in the guts and then slugged him square on the chin. He collapsed on the piss-stained floor. "Ow. Oh, mother of Christ. Oof."

We pushed through the door and pushed through the celebrating crowd. It was a drunken mess outside. Next to a concession stand, my father saw a ten-pound bag of salted peanuts in the shell. He scooped it up. We found our car in the muni lot and honked and drove the best we could out of there, my father shouting, "Move it, asshole!" at all the staggering fans jamming the lot and the streets outside.

I pulled the map out of the glove box and turned on the overhead light. I directed my father through the streets.

Left here.

Right here.

A few more blocks. Keep going.

We're here.

We got out of the car. I ran to the door of the dog pound, fumbled with the key, dropped it, and finally stuck it in the keyhole. I opened the door and pushed inside, my father right behind me with a baseball bat in his hand.

The lights were off. I flipped them on. Like all the other dog pounds we'd been to, it was a mess. A sign on the wall announced, "THIS IS A <u>KILL</u> SHELTER."

My father did what he'd done in the previous places and opened the cages, releasing strays who quickly phased back over to being human again.

I walked along looking furiously for her. "Katie!" I shouted. "Katie!"

I found her.

She was human. She was curled up inside the cage, her knees tucked in to nearly her chin. She was dressed in a dirty pair of sweats, dingy gray, shot full of holes and stained horribly. Her feet were calloused and dirty and bare. Her hair was dingy and matted. She was moaning. She'd soiled herself.

I opened the cage and pulled her out as gently as I could. She was awake, but she wouldn't look at me. "Leave me," she said.

"No," I said.

"Please. Leave me. They killed her. They killed my sweet dog. The one inside me. They killed her."

"I won't leave you."

I slipped my arms underneath her and lifted her up. She was light as a feather. There was nothing to her. Nothing but skin and bones. She gave off an odor that was like death itself, pungent and penetrating. Tears poured down her cheeks. "I'm sorry."

"No, I'm sorry. I failed you. I'm sorry I was too late to save your dog, the one inside you. She was a good dog. She was the best dog."

She cried out in pain. She wouldn't look at me still. I carried her toward the door. My father noticed and grabbed the door for me. He ran over to the car and I slipped into the back bench seat with Katie. I held her while my father drove. She wept.

I carried her inside the house and down to the bathroom. I sat her down on the toilet. I put in the plug and ran the bathwater. I put in some shampoo to make it foam a bit.

When the tub was full, I turned to her and said, "Do you trust me?"

"Yes," she said. "I trust you."

I carefully unzipped her filthy sweatshirt. She had nothing on underneath. She was all ribs. Her tiny breasts sagged. I took off the sweatshirt and tossed it on the floor. I had her stand up and pulled down her filthy sweatpants. She had on nothing underneath them. She stepped out of one side and then the other. I tossed them next to the sweatshirt. I cleaned up her backside with wads of toilet paper and flushed them down the toilet. "I'm sorry," she said. I tried to clean her up with a soapy washcloth. She tolerated it, her eyes closed. She trembled a bit.

"I want you to get in the tub," I said.

"I don't think I can," she said.

So I lifted her up and placed her as gently as I could in the tub. I washed her. I shampooed her hair twice. I clipped her nails and scrubbed the dirt away. I emptied the tub and refilled it. I sat with her while she soaked. I lit the candles and turned out the lights.

She said, after a lengthy silence, "I knew you'd come for me."

"That's what friends do," I said.

I drained the tub and dried her off with the towels I'd set aside for her. I wrapped her hair in a towel.

"I'm not going to put that on again," she said, pointing over at her sweatsuit.

"I'll get you something." I went into my closet and found a St. Sebastian's gym t-shirt and shorts.

When I came back in, she said, "This isn't the way I imagined you seeing me naked for the first time."

I blushed a bit and looked away.

"I must look terrible," she said.

"You're beautiful. And I'll fight anyone who says otherwise."

She bowed down a bit and I took the towel off her head. I helped her put on the t-shirt and shorts. She lost her balance and nearly fell. I caught her in my arms. I held her. I carried her into the bedroom and put her into my bed. I went into the bathroom and blew out all the candles. I grabbed an old sleeping bag from inside my closet. It had pictures of pheasants printed all over it. I rolled it out on the floor next to the bed. I turned off the light. I took off my pants and got inside the sleeping bag. "Don't step on me if you get up in the middle of the night."

"Okay," she said.

"I'm right here."

"I can sleep on the floor."

"You've done enough of that."

"I don't want to sleep. I have to dream as a person, not as a dog," Katie said. "It hurts too much to dream as a person."

"We'll dream together," I said, reaching up to the bed and taking her hand. "We'll share the pain. We'll find the good things, too. I promise. I won't leave you. I'm in this for the duration."

We held hands until we each fell asleep.

In the dream we had together, we were in a drafty house in the middle of the suburbs. Outside, there was a vast black storm. Whirling in the wind was black dirt, bugs, and bark stripped from trees. Some bugs, dirt and bark came in under the door. We stuffed a towel under it. Some leaked in through the window. We stuffed wet paper towels to stop it. It came in through the drain pipes, and we stuffed a sock in each one. We retreated to a bedroom and closed the door and listened to the dirt, bugs and bark pummel the house, clattering against windows and doors.

The roof lifted off. We watched it rise higher and higher and then came the crawling bugs and bark and dirt. Katie screamed.

I woke up. I got up to my knees and shook her awake. "You see?" she went.

"What was that?"

"It's the dream I've had, ever since I was a child. I ruined my family."

"It's about losing your home."

"That's my house. From when I was a kid."

"Where were your parents? Your little brother? Your little sister?"

"My sister? How did you know about my little sister?" she asked suspiciously.

"I don't know."

"You don't know? You named your daughter after her."

"I don't know why I did that. I liked the name."

"We're going to talk about it. Sooner rather than later." She sat up in bed. "What time is it? Is it time to get up?"

"Yes," my mother said from the doorway. She was a wisp. Almost not there. "It's time. Come with me." She turned and walked away.

"I'm scared," Katie said.

"It's okay. She's my mother. She likes you."

"Did she say that?"

"I'm pretty sure she did."

"Pretty sure."

"I'm certain she likes you." I turned my head and shouted, "Mom? Mom, do you like Katie?"

"Of course I like Katie!" my mother called back. "Hurry up. It's time. Get in here."

We entered the kitchen on tiptoe. Me, in my tightie-whities and black t-shirt. Katie, in my old gym uniform. We held hands.

My mother stood next to the sink. The doors underneath were open. "Down you go," my mother said.

"Mrs. Derleth?"

"Please. Call me Marie."

"Marie? What's down there?"

"It's just a good, old-fashioned existential void. Nothing to write home about." My mother smiled at the two of us. "Would you believe that I was happy in this house? I was." She looked around. "So, this is the last time you'll see me."

"What?" I went.

"I'm finished after this. Done. I'll move along to whatever's next."

"What about dad?"

"Oh, he'll be okay. I think he needed this little adventure, don't you? He needed to find out that he wasn't the jerk that he was pretending to be. Maybe be the good guy for once."

"I guess so."

"Don't you like him now?"

"I guess I do."

"See? Now come here and give your mother a hug."

"I thought we weren't the hugging types?"

"There's always an exception, isn't there?" I gave my mother a hug. She was all right, my mother. "You're a good boy," she said. She called over Katie, and whispered something in her ear. Katie nodded her head. "I need you both to sit on the ledge there," my mother said. We sat down, our legs dangling out into the existential void. "Pretend like one of you is wearing a parachute and needs the other to hold onto you to survive." We wrapped our arms around each other. "Take care of my boy," she said, and gave us a shove.

We fell. And fell.

THE EIGHT STEPS

1. We were back in the desert. In Iraq. Where else would we end up in an existential void?

We were sitting on the desert floor, our backs up against a conex box. I had a sketch pad in my hand. I was finishing up a drawing of Katie. I was just about it tear it off the pad and hand it to her. I stuck the pencil in my teeth and started to take it off the pad.

"Right here," Katie said. "This moment? This is when you should have kissed me the first time." She pointed at the drawing. "You know how sexy this is? I mean, have you seen *Titanic*?"

I spat out the pencil. "Oh, shit. Are you kidding me? Why didn't you tell me?"

"I'm telling you now, stupid."

I put the sketch pad aside. I scrambled to my knees. So did she. I unsnapped her chin strap and carefully lifted the kevlar off her head. I took off my helmet and set it aside. I leaned in too quickly and I nearly chipped one of her teeth.

"Too eager at seventeen," Katie said after we indulged in a long, lingering kiss. "Still, a pretty good first effort." She picked up the helmet and put it back on. "Let's go back earlier though." She spun her finger around and we clicked over to an earlier time.

2. I was sitting in the dee-fac, my serving tray pushed aside. I was drawing a scene I remembered from the original *Star Trek*, the one with Shatner as Captain Kirk. Kirk was acting heavily in my comic. I knew someone was sitting across from me, but I didn't want to look up. Usually, it was Squid, who always asked the same question. "What're you drawing?"

"What're you drawing?" a female voice asked.

I looked up and PFC Tanaka, the new soldier in the unit, was sitting across from me.

"Hi, Tanaka," I said. "It's James T. Kirk. He's ready to emote the shit out of this scene."

"Cool," she said. "You ever think about doing a graphic novel?"

"I'd need someone to write it. I'm no good at the writing parts."

"Well then. You're in luck." She outlined her ideas for a graphic novel. It was all so visual. It was like she was lighting up parts of my brain that I didn't know could be lit. She told me a tale about surfers in San Pedro, California who, at night, transformed into stray dogs and roamed the streets, protecting the innocent. While she spoke, I drew what I saw in my head. It was a girl in a wetsuit running across a beach in one panel and in the next she was a golden retriever. No transformation. Click, click. Like a PowerPoint slide. I spun it around and slid it across the table to her.

"That's it," she said, excitement trembling in her throat. "That's what I see in my head."

"I'll have to go to San Pedro so I can see the place for myself," I said. "Take photos. Draw it over and over."

"Yes. Totally." She smiled at me. She quickly got up, sat next to me and studied my Captain Kirk rendering. "Do you ever draw any *Star Wars* stuff?"

That's when we had our epic *Star Trek* versus *Star Wars* argument. We each thought we'd won. When I got back to my conex box and took off my gear, Squid asked me where I'd been. I told him about the argument with Tanaka. I didn't tell him about the graphic novel. That was between her and me.

"You must like her," he said.

"Why do you say that?"

"Because this is the first time I've ever seen you smile."

"It's not like that," I said.

Clearly, it was like that.

3. And then we were back in the dee-fac. Katie and I sat together watching one of the plasma TVs. It was a sitcom that starred my father called, *That Darned Dad.* The theme song went, "He's slightly sexist and slightly sad; He doesn't think much, he's that darned dad!"

We watched Larry bickering with his ghost wife, Marie, as canned laughter washed over the soundtrack.

"Come on, Larry!" Marie said, her fists on her hips. "You gotta do something about this gosh-darned existential void under the kitchen sink!"

Larry was hiding behind the sports section of the *Plain Dealer*. In gigantic type on the cover was "CAVS WIN NBA CHAMPIONSHIP." In smaller type: "EARTH TEMPORARILY TILTS OFF AXIS." "Don't worry about it, Marie. I gotta guy coming over." He flipped to the next page. Ding-dong went the doorbell. "I'll get it," Larry said, setting down the paper. "That's gotta be him."

A man with an excess of gray-white hair piled atop his head walked in. He had an unlit briar clenched in his teeth. He wore a tweed jacket with elbow patches, a black mock turtleneck, pressed jeans, and sandals with sweatsocks. "I'm here about your little problem," the man said. "Doctor Bertie. I believe your son contacted me on the phone?"

"Yes! At last!" Larry shook Doctor Bertie's hand. It was a good double-pumper.

Doctor Bertie shook the hurt out of his hand and then watched as Larry blinked in and out of existence. "I see the problem here. You suffer from what we call Metaphysical Adjustment Disorder, or MAD. Good thing you called me. Seems that I got here in the nick of time!"

"What do I need to do, Doc?" Larry asked him. "You gotta help me! I could wink out of existence at any moment."

"Hey!" Marie shouted from the kitchen. "I thought you were gonna fix the sink!"

"I'm not a plumber, madam," Doctor Bertie said. "I'm a philosopher."

"Nag, nag, nag!" Larry said to howls of artificial laughter.

"Come take a look anyway," Marie said, opening the doors beneath the sink.

"Fascinating!" Doctor Bertie said, quickly making his way to the kitchen sink and crouching down.

"Hey! What about me?" Larry shouted. He shorted out again and winked back into existence.

"This, I believe, is the cause of your problem," Doctor Bertie said, standing up. He took the pipe out of his mouth and placed it in his pocket. "What have you been doing in this house to disrupt the order of the universe?"

"I haven't done nothing!" Larry shouted. "Why is it always me getting screwed? Huh? I wanna know the answer to that question, Doctor Smartypants!"

Doctor Bertie picked up the book leaning against the counter: *Will It Waffle? A Guide to Waffle Cookery* by Lowell Thomas. He flipped through it. "My God, man! What sort of insanity is this?"

"Whatta y'mean?" Larry asked, to hails of artificial laughter.

"I mean, this book is a mockery of the natural order of things. This is your problem, right here."

"I gotta admit, I have no idea what you're talking about," Larry said.

"I understand," Marie said.

Doctor Bertie nodded appreciatively at Marie. "Perhaps your late wife can explain this to you."

"Define 'waffle,'" Marie said.

"Precisely," Doctor Bertie said.

"What?" Larry went, clearly in mental and physical agony as he dropped to the floor and buzzed on and off. The laugh track went wild.

"A waffle is a crisp, sweet cake made in a waffle iron and served with butter and syrup," Doctor Bertie said. "It is NOT savory! This book and your actions caused a rift in reality itself." Doctor Bertie reached into his pocket and produced a lighter. He set the book on fire and put it in the sink. The book quickly turned into delicate flakes of ash that danced above the sink before breaking apart.

The pipes, wastepaper basket and Bon Ami appeared where the void had once been.

Larry stood up and patted his chest. He poked his cheeks with his index fingers. He grabbed at his thighs with his hands. "I'm whole again!" he declared.

Marie walked over to him, took him into her arms, dipped him and gave him a big smooch as the synthetic audience ooohed and awww-ed. "Goodbye, Larry," she said, letting him go. Larry dropped to the floor. "I love you, you dope." She faded out of existence.

"Marie!" Larry shouted.

"Now, I believe there was the matter of my fee." Doctor Bertie lit his pipe and took a couple of puffs.

"Fee?" Larry went, his eyes filled with tears. "Oh," he said meekly. "Right." He left the room and came back with a ten-pound bag of peanuts.

The philosopher hugged the bag to his chest. "I'm going to be naughty tonight," he said, as the laugh track chortled. He left through the front door.

"Marie?" Larry went, plaintively. "Marie?"

The screen faded and a commercial came on for Amphion B. "Feeling stressed by life?" the voiceover asked, as a computer animated man made of clear plastic rolled on the ground, hugging his knees, his torso filled with electricity. "Try Amphion B! Amphion B gives you a heightened lack of awareness of your situation in life. Ask your doctor today about Amphion B!"

4. Katie and I were in a commandeered conex box. We'd foraged art supplies and a table with a flat enough surface that it could be used as a drafting table. We foraged lights. We had a fan set up by the door, but it was still steaming hot in there and stuffy. We took turns swigging out of large bottles of water. We both leaned on the drafting table, sweat dripping down onto the pages. She was writing words down along with stick figures showing vaguely what the characters should be doing. I was sketching quickly, but with authority. It was heady.

I turned to her and asked, "Is this a real memory?"

"Yes and no. We never got this far originally. We talked about it, but we never actually set up in one of the empty conex boxes."

"So this is new?"

"It's new and it's old," she said. She kissed me on the cheek and I blushed. "It's what we talked about doing, and now we're doing it. For real. In the past. It's exciting, isn't it?"

"It's exciting," I agreed. "This existential void is kind of all right."

My hands weren't shaking. Not at all.

5. We were in the dee-fac again. We walked in together. Inside, there was everyone in headquarters and headquarters company. They were pounding on the tables, facing a small stage. On the stage was Fun Boss Todd, a robust retired chief petty officer in the Navy, who was now working as a non-appropriated fund employee of the Army at FOB Eagle. He was there, as his job title implied, to make us have fun. He was brutal about it.

Fun Boss Todd was standing next to a karaoke machine. Lights flashed on it. He waved a microphone in the air, and then brought it down to his enormous, cement block head to intone, "Who's next!" His voice boomed through the dee-fac. The scent of chili mac was wafting through the air. Fun Boss Todd's t-shirt said in bright red letters, "FUN BOSS." "Oh, ho-ho! Look who we have here! It's my favorite little Asian girl and her smiling boyfriend, the combat cartoonist! If we all clap loud enough, I bet we can make these two lovebirds sing a song! What do you say? Let's give them a big INFANTRY HOO-AH!"

"HOO-AH!" the entire company boomed out. They slapped the tables louder.

Katie and I ran up to the stage. "Beat it, Fun Boss Todd," Katie said. He handed Katie the microphone, and bowed. "This one goes out to headquarters and headquarters company!" Katie said, to the accompaniment of cheers and hoo-ahs. She scrolled through the choices and found one to her liking. "Sing along, if you dare," she shouted into the mic.

Katie and I sang, as the words scrolled on the screen:

Yeah
You are my fire
The one desire
Believe when I say
I want it that way
But we are two worlds apart
Can't reach to your heart
When you say
That I want it that way

When we were done with the song, Katie said, "Top that," and dropped the mic to the dee-fac floor. She took off her kevlar and whipped it into the crowd, hitting Doc on the bridge of his nose. She grabbed me around the neck and kissed me in front of everyone. They all went crazy, flipping over tables and benches, tossing condiment bottles at each other.

We walked out together, holding hands.

"Is this just wish-fulfillment?" I asked her, outside in the one-hundred degree heat.

"Sure," she said. "But it's real, too. I can feel it."

6. But then there was the part we couldn't change. I looked around. I was in the back of the deuce-and-a-half, scanning the horizon. Katie was in the front, assistant fifty cal gunner for Crabby, who wasn't paying any attention. He was smoking a cigarette, supremely bored, even though we knew that we had enemy combatants hiding in the area.

The rocket was in the air, heading directly for Katie. She had to live. There was no way I could live if she died. So I leapt over and pushed her to the truck bed, my momentum taking me over toward Crabby, shouldering him out of the way.

And the idea to catch the rocket came into my head. I'd catch it and toss it away, where it wouldn't hurt anyone. It was such a good idea. I mean, the rocket seemed pretty catchable, like a soft pass from Tim Couch.

It turned out not to be that catchable. It ricochetted off my body armor and hit me square in the forehead, but didn't explode for some reason. It fluttered into the sky. I watched it as I lay on the ground. I'd somehow ended up there on the sand, staring into the superheated air. I was calm. The world seemed so pretty in that moment. The rocket popped. A puff of white smoke drifted away.

I heard the fifty cal fire.

Doc was the first one to appear in my line of vision. "Holy shit, dude. That was awesome," he said.

"Thanks," I said.

"I knew volunteering for this mission would pay off."

"Glad to be of service," I said.

He took off my kevlar and set it aside. "Man, I think your skull is cracked. You won't live through golden hour, that's for sure." He smirked. "What a fuck-tard!"

"Fix him!" Katie shrieked. "Fix him, or I swear I'll fucking kill you!"

"His head's broken," Doc said. "He's a dead man." He stood up. "Fucking awesome."

Katie dropped to her knees. "This wasn't supposed to happen again. Why'd you do it? Why?"

"It's okay," I said. "Everything is fine." The world began to spin a bit.

"I will find you," Katie said. "This time I'll find you."

I could hear a helicopter off in the distance. "They're coming for me. It'll be okay. Look for me at the Navy hospital in Illinois." I had a splitting headache. Literally, I realized. I laughed. I was going to explain the joke to Katie, but she was fading away.

"My love is toxic," she said. I felt her fingers on my jugular. "That's two people I've killed, just by loving..."

"Wait," I said. "What?"

7. I was back in the void, wandering alone in pitch-black darkness. I was at the bottom of the void. I had to be. There was a floor to walk on. I could hear my footsteps echo. Finally, I saw a light. At first, it was a pinprick. But as I walked toward it, it expanded.

I was standing on someone's yard in suburbia. There were tall palm trees as high as the sky and houses with stucco and arches. The roofs were covered in red tile. A tree with purple flowers rustled in a breeze that smelled like the ocean. A soccer ball rolled up to me. I stopped it with my foot, which was covered over in a brown, suede combat boot. I was still in uniform. Thankfully, I hadn't brought my busted M16 with me, or someone would have called the police. I reached up and my head was sticky with dried blood.

"You okay, mister?" a kid asked me.

"I'm fine," I said.

"Because I think you're bleeding or something," he said.

"I think it's stopped," I said.

"You in the Army or something?"

"Or something," I said.

"I gotta go." He ran off with the soccer ball. I watched the kids play for a while.

Across the street was a cul-de-sac with more Spanish-type homes. At the far end of the cul-de-sac was a home not in the same style as the rest of the houses. It was Katie's house. I recognized it from our dream.

I saw two little girls standing on the other side of the road, at our end of the cul-de-sac. The older girl stood watching the soccer game. The smaller girl was trying to get her attention. "Look at me, Katie! Look at me!" She danced around her older sister.

"Go home, Annie! Quit bugging me!" Katie said. "Scoot!"

"You're not allowed to cross the street. It's too dangerous," Annie said.

"I know that. You don't think I know that?"

"Look at me, Katie." The little girl danced around in the grass and then tried to stand on her head. She flopped over.

"Go home!" Katie shouted at her.

"You wanna play soccer, but you're not allowed to cross the street," Annie said, with a little taunt in her voice.

"Oh, yeah? Watch me!" Katie said. She dashed across the street and made it to the other side.

I realized that the adult Katie was standing next to me, also in uniform. "No!" she screamed, but Annie ran across anyway. A rust-eaten Geo Metro seemingly appeared out of nowhere and hit the little girl. A woman, clearly drunk, staggered out of the car. She peered over at the crowd of children who'd stopped playing soccer. They were all staring at her. She panicked, got back in the car, backed up and then drove around the little girl.

Katie and I ran over.

Little Katie was already on her knees in the street, holding her sister in her arms. "Annie! Annie, wake up!"

"It's okay, Katie," Annie said. "Everything is fine. I'm sorry. I'm so sorry."

We watched Annie die in little Katie's arms. We stepped back. The surviving sibling was numb. We watched the police arrive. We watched the ambulance come. We saw Katie's parents arrive. We saw them break down.

Katie the soldier turned to me and said, "I wish that she was still alive…" She screamed at the top of her lungs, long and loud. When she was done she said bitterly, "Do you see what wishing does? It does nothing!"

8. And then we were in little Katie's room. The one she'd shared with Annie. The top bunk was empty. A Hello Kitty night light illuminated the room. A My Little Pony alarm clock told us it was ten after midnight.

Little Katie was numb. She still hadn't cried. She was wide awake. "Who are you?" she asked us.

"Tell her," I told Katie.

"I'm you," Katie said.

"I'm a soldier?"

"Yes. You will be."

"Why?"

"Because we had to get away. From here. From this."

"Who's he?"

"He's our boyfriend."

"Why's his head so bloody?"

"Because he's sorta stupid. But we love him anyway."

"Okay. I guess he's kinda cute," she said. "Why can't I cry?"

"You will," Katie said. "You'll cry for a long time and you won't be able to stop. You'll think it's the worst thing that ever happened, until this stupid, stupid man tries to catch a rocket that was meant for you. Then you can't decide which is worse."

"I killed her," little Katie said. The words choked in her throat.

"Tell her," I said. "Tell her now."

Katie knelt beside the bed. She took her own hand. The little girl's hand. "You didn't kill her. That drunk lady did."

"Forgive her," I said.

"What?" they both said, turning toward me.

"She deserves your compassion," I said. "The same compassion you give everyone but yourself. It wasn't your fault. You just said so. You have to forgive her. You have to forgive yourself."

The soldier hugged the little girl. "So what do you think? Makes sense?"

"Makes sense," the little girl said.

Katie the soldier stood up and walked over to me. She took my hand. "It's time to go back," she said.

HAPPINESS

We awoke on my bed in my father's house. We were fully dressed, save for our shoes. I blinked the sleep out of my eyes and sat up. Katie looked at me and said, "Why do you have a beard?"

I felt my face. It was a very full beard. Bushy. I had on tight jeans that didn't quite make it all the way down to my ankles, and a soft plaid shirt. I reached up and instinctively touched my forehead scar. That was still there. Then I kept feeling upward and discovered that I had tied my long hair into a knot on the top of my head. "Oh, no."

I looked at what Katie was wearing. She had on black tights and a plaid skirt. She wore a white t-shirt with a logo for Cuyahoga Comics on it. I'd drawn it. I recognized my artwork. Her hair was red at the top and blonde toward the tips and hung past her shoulders. She had on a knit cap that looked like it was made by someone's grandma and a pair of black plastic sunglasses rested on her nose. She wore blood-red lipstick. We swung our feet out of bed and then walked over to the bathroom together and looked into the mirror. Katie whipped off the sunglasses and tossed them aside.

"We're hipsters!" we both shouted in horror.

"That beard's gotta come off," Katie said quickly.

"Today," I said. "And you gotta dye your hair back to..."

"Consider it done," she said. She pulled off the knit cap with her left hand. That's when she noticed the rings on her ring finger. There was a tasteful little engagement ring and a wedding band. She grabbed my left hand. There was a black band on my ring finger. "We're married."

"I'm sure it'll come back to us."

"Yes, and there's something else. Someone else."

I turned around just as our daughter ran into the bathroom. She was dressed up like Princess Leia from the original movie. I picked her up and held her up with my left arm. "How's it going, sugar pie?" I asked her. She had one brown eye and one blue eye, just like her mother.

"Grandpa's cheating," she said.

"Of course he is," I said. "Grandpa always cheats. What's he cheating at today?"

"Crazy eights," she said.

Katie took her out of my grasp and hugged her. "That Grandpa. He's always up to no good. I don't know why you want to come over."

"It's because Grandpa," I said, pinching our little girl's cheeks, "is always making waffles."

"Grandpa says you need a shave and a haircut," our daughter Annie said. Katie let her back down to the floor.

"Even a broken clock is right twice a day," I said.

We walked out and sat on my mother's ratty sofa. The TV was on. The Indians were playing a day game. It was Sunday. They were at home. They were running away with the division, it looked like. I heard my father talking to someone on the phone in the kitchen.

"I told you! They make good money, my son and his lovely bride. They're not fooling around with those comics. There's a lot of money in them. More than he would have made being a stone mason like his old man." He stopped talking for a moment. He started up again. "No, it's some crazy crap about people becoming dogs, or something. Takes place in Cleveland. Yeah, and I'm in it, too. Or at least the father he drew looks a lot like me. They even put you in it, Joe. So look. I'll be down there later on to pay my tab, after they leave for the day. They're in his bedroom taking a nap while I entertain my granddaughter. She's the spitting image of Marie, God rest her soul. I'm glad she hung on long enough to see her born." He peered around the corner and saw us sitting there. "I gotta go. They're up." He rolled his eyes. "I swear to you, I have the money for my tab, Joe. Don't sweat it. Gotta go." He hung up the phone. He wandered out into the living room and sat down on his barcalounger.

"I told on you, Grandpa," Annie said. She walked over to his chair and made a face at him.

He made a mock sad face. "Oh, Grandpa's in trouble, is he?"

"You betcha," Annie said.

"I wonder what I could do to get out of trouble?" my father asked, rolling his eyes dramatically.

"Why are you a better grandparent than you ever were a parent?" I asked him.

"Practice," he said. "Plus, she's cuter than you were. By far. Your papa was, how to put this kindly? Not a good looking kid," my father told Annie.

Annie said, "Nah-uh."

"Oh, I'm afraid that's the truth, sweetie," my father said. "I imagine that someone in this house wants waffles."

"You imagine right," Katie said.

"Then I guess I better get to work," my father said. Annie flew into the kitchen ahead of him. He paused in front of me, blocking my view of the TV. "Son, do you think you could see fit to, um, lend your old man a cee-note?"

"Jeez, dad. What've you been drinking at Joe's? Top shelf swill?" I pulled out my wallet and it was filled with money. More money than I'd ever seen in my life. I gave Katie a panicked look. She looked equally panicked and quickly pulled out some bills and gave them to my father. I put away the wallet.

"This is too generous," my father said, taking the cash, counting it quickly, and stashing it in his front pocket.

"Don't worry about it, dad," I said.

"Get you anything?" he asked. "While I'm in the kitchen?"

"Mustard and pickle sandwich?"

My father and I both laughed.

As Katie and I sat on the sofa, paying no attention to the game on the TV, our life since the Army came flooding back to us. How she took care of me after I got out of the Navy hospital. How we took over an old comic book shop down in the Flats using a VA loan. How we got married at St. Sebastian's and had our reception at the guild hall while Buddy Riccardo and his International Band played. How we built-up a business together. How during the evenings, we made our comics, and sold them during the day. How we hired our fellow veterans as the business grew, and turned over most of the daily operations to an eccentric Marine who went by the moniker, "El Chicharrón." How our comics caught on, first in our store, and then in other stores through word of mouth, and then the Internet. How we spent our days after that creating an entire world on the page. Together. We remembered Annie's birth. We remembered bringing her out to California to meet her grandmother and her uncle. And her step-grandfather, the dentist. Katie taught me how to surf. We had our ups and downs, but mostly everything was good. We followed the dream path. I loved our work and our life together. That's when it hit me. I whispered into Katie's ear, "Holy shit. We're happy."

"I know," she said, sounding just as stupefied as I was.

Annie ran into the room with a plate and showed it to us. On it was a waffle with a smile made out of whipped cream and eyes made out of strawberries.

"You gonna eat that, or admire it?" my father shouted.

About the author...

I was born in Ohio, in a town just outside of Cleveland, a few days after Christmas 1963. My memories of Cleveland are of filthy snow, smoky bowling alleys and banged knees turned crusty-scabby. My family moved around a lot when I was a kid. We ended up dropping roots in Sarasota, Florida.

I worked in restaurants for seven years, from my teens up through my early twenties. I tried to master my anxiety, my panic, my sense of impending failure. I failed.

I was working grill at a Steak n Shake in Gainesville, Florida, and contemplating flunking out of college. The guy who was working the drive-through asked me if that was my bitching motorcycle parked under the awning next to the picnic tables. I said yes. The meat on the grill sizzled. I imagined that it was talking to me. I'd been working graveyard four years, and going to school full-time. He told me about tanker boots, very cool, which featured a leather strap that circled around your ankle. He told me that the army gives that kind of cool shit away. The cock at the Vietnamese restaurant next door crowed three times. A car drove past on 13th Street dragging a muffler. Sparks. The guy told me that he was going to join the army, probably tomorrow. I went with him to the recruiter's office--unimpeded by lack of sleep.

The army had three very important questions to ask before allowing me to join: 1. Are you a communist? 2. Are you a homosexual? 3. Are you plotting to overthrow the United States government? I answered "no" to all three questions. As luck would have it, there wasn't a question four: Are you nuts? I started out as a PFC in September 1987 and ended up—4 years, 2 months and 13 days later—a Spec-4.

I spent a couple of years in the reserves, too.

My little sister Nancy was gunned down at a Pizza Hut restaurant in Brandon, Florida shortly after midnight on May 27, 1992—my mother's 56th birthday. As a result, my family disintegrated. It's all very tragic.

Somewhere in there, I went back to school and got an **MFA at the University of Florida**. I wrote junk mail for a while, mostly hospital newsletters. One of the articles I wrote was "'Mommy, I don't feel so good': What to do when your child has the sniffles." Another had to do with a whirling bathtub and its the miraculous effects on oldsters at the Bohemian Home for the Aged. I wrote a few articles for credit card inserts, too, encouraging people to spend, spend, spend. I quit.

I took electronic publishing courses for a time so I could collect the rest of my GI Bill. Then I taught at a community college. I kept chewing on life, even though it had lost its flavor. I got married. I got divorced.

In 2014, I was in a motorcycle accident. I braked to avoid hitting a deer in the road, flew over the handlebars of a vintage BMW, and landed on my left shoulder and head. I was wearing a helmet. I shattered my clavicle and broke seven ribs. I had to have surgery. For about a year afterward, I couldn't tell the difference between dreams and reality. I still can't remember a lot of things since that day. I've forgotten names, people and entire years. Maybe that's for the best. I'm happier.

I'm a federal employee, and about four years away from a retirement.

The book I'm known for, if I'm known at all, is *Small Town Punk*. There are others. All proceeds from sales of my books go into the John L. Sheppard Pre-Memorial Beer Fund.

By John L. Sheppard

www.johnlsheppard.com